I0683830

FreeForm: Resumed

FreeForm, Volume 3

Orrin Jason Bradford

Published by Porpoise Publishing, 2019.

FreeForm: Resumed

Orrin Jason Bradford

The only solution to humanity's plight is itself part of the problem

Despite appearances, TJ—now Private First Class Todd John Jacobs—has little in common with his fellow rangers. After all, there's a world of difference between blending in and fitting in. When a military assignment in Iraq goes horribly wrong, will this outsider's differences prove a boon or a blight? Civilization, itself, may rest upon the shoulders of one man...who isn't a man at all.

Colonel Stanwick knows the truth about Jacobs and aims to eliminate FreeForm by leveraging that knowledge...but can a shapeshifter be bent to a mere mortal's will? Fighting fire with fire could lead to an inferno that swallows the globe.

Graver still, a reanimated Homlin has grown increasingly powerful and evil as Val as his revived plot nears fruition. Under the tutelage of the artificial intelligence, Aeo, Val is positioned to forge connections with those that rule the planet, at least for now. But all too soon, Earth's natives may find themselves longing for a ruthless cartel's comparative mercy. With James Stepp falling into old habits, paths will cross as pivotal pieces connect. Things are coming to a head...and it isn't human.

Next--*FreeForm: New Birth*

Outside Fallujah

The vibration and rocking of the helicopter combined with the moonless night sky to lull Sergeant Todd John Jacobs into a semi-trance. So much had happened in the past six months since graduating from Ranger school, most of which he still didn't fully understand. The mysterious man who'd met him as he left the graduation stage turned out to be Lieutenant Phillip Ackerson, or Jersey as he preferred to be called. Jersey, an Army officer assigned to special duty with the CIA, had all but hogtied him. He claimed he was there to offer Todd his next assignment per their commander in chief, the President of the United States. That job had turned out to be six more months of rigorous training and intel briefings that had eventually led to tonight's mission somewhere in the vicinity of Fallujah, Iraq.

He shook himself awake as he heard the order on his headset, "Five minutes till drop off. Get ready." As Todd looked around, he could just make out James, the pilot, and his co-pilot whose name Todd couldn't remember in front with the crew chief and a door gunner seated behind them. Farther to his right, he saw the outline of Jersey. He knew the other two men assigned to the mission were seated behind the Lieutenant on the opposite side of the helicopter. Jasper Mullins was a good ole boy from the south, so Todd found they had a natural affinity for each other. He found the shorter man, Dewey Stalins, more abrasive and eager to start a fight, so he'd made it a point to stay out of Dewey's way.

Todd rubbed the smooth metal of his M4 weapon sitting in his lap. He found it comforting and hoped the silencer would allow them an easy in and out if he ended up needing to use it. The weight of the backpack on his shoulders meant it was time for action—the part of military life he loved. Jersey reached over and gave a thumbs up. Todd returned the gesture. The second the aircraft hit the ground they would be running.

Todd felt the aircraft flare, settle, and the doors opened. He jumped out into the pitch blackness of a moonless night, ran about fifty feet and dropped to the ground. The helicopter departed without ever coming to a full stop. Todd stood up, adjusting his night vision goggles even though he didn't need them and looked around. It was important to play the role that he was just like the other soldiers. Three other figures also stood up. The one nearest to him pointed in a direction to the south and started off in a fast jog. The other two moved to his sides and matched stride, with Todd taking up the rear. They ran like this for what Todd calculated to be three-quarters of a mile, putting them a quarter mile from the village that was just over the rise in front of them.

Jersey, in the lead, signaled to stop and then kneeled. Todd, Jasper, and Dewey caught up and kneeled beside him. "Damn, this is getting harder every mission," Jersey whispered even though he didn't appear to be at all winded. "I need to get out of this business. All right guys, you know the drill. Refresh if needed and check your weapons and gear. Let's get in there as planned, snatch the package, and get out without anyone knowing what hit them. Any questions?"

Todd looked around. No one had any. Jersey nodded and moved off in the direction of the village. Everyone else walked up to a line position and spread out. As they got closer to the village, Todd could see the wall around it and the doorway of the building they were to go through. According to their intel, the door would be unlocked for them, and someone would lead them to the location of the package.

As the team approached the building, Todd noticed some lights in the distance to the west of their position but decided they were probably just goat herders. As he drew nearer to their target, he started having tremors of an odd, yet vaguely familiar feeling which grew stronger the closer he got to the building. What the hell was going on? He'd never felt anything like this on his previous training missions. Maybe those lights weren't goat herders after all.

The creaking of the door cut through the silence of the night as Jersey pushed it open, but before he could enter through it, a man dressed in traditional Arab garb stepped out from the darkness and started firing, hitting Jersey and Dewey. Todd jumped forward and struck the man in the head with the butt of his gun. He yelled for Jasper to secure the area and bolted through the door. Sensing two men on the other side of the door, he cut them both down before they had a chance to react.

Todd paused a moment leaning against one wall, allowing his heightened senses to scan the area. Detecting no one else close by, he signaled for Jasper to bring in their fallen team members. Glancing at Dewey's bloody pulp of a head, Todd knew he couldn't be helped. He started to turn his attention to Jersey who'd been hit in the side, but Jasper was already applying pressure to the wound. Todd grabbed the unconscious Arab and slapped his face several times to revive him. The man's eyes shot open. Apparently, he'd only been pretending to be unconscious.

Todd forced the barrel of the M4 into the man's mouth. "What the hell happened? Why did you shoot at us?" he screamed. The man glared back, defiantly refusing to talk. "So, that's the way you want to play this?" Todd said between clenched teeth. He yanked the gun barrel from the man's mouth and shot off the big toe of his left foot. The man screamed, his eyes growing wide with pain and fear.

"Let's try that again," Todd said. "Why are you shooting at us? You were supposed to help." The man shook his head and spat at him. Todd shrugged, pointed his weapon at the other foot and shot off the other big toe. The man screamed even louder this time. "Okay, one last chance," Todd said as he pointed the gun at the man's crotch. That did the trick.

"Please, no more. I'll talk...please," the man pleaded with a thick accent. After another moment, he continued. "We got the word you were coming. We were ordered to set a trap. Please, I was only following orders."

"That's what they always say," Todd replied. He thought about smacking his captive in the head again but paused to assess the situation first. "Damn, now what do we do?"

"Todd, we have to get out of here," Jersey answered him from where he was lying on the floor, a pool of blood beginning to form despite Jasper's pressure.

"The hell with that. We haven't completed our mission yet. We're not leaving until we've recovered the package, dead or alive."

"We've obviously been made," Jersey said, wincing in pain. "It's time to scrub the mission."

Todd leaned over him and tore the fabric away from the shoulder of his shirt where the bullet had entered. "It's just a flesh wound. Trust me. I can handle this. It's what I've been made for," Todd said. He turned to Jasper. "Take care of him. Keep pressure on the wound and stay alert. There may be others around. Contact me on the headset if things change."

"Will do," Jasper replied, not questioning Todd's self-proclaimed authority.

"This asshole and I are going to take a walk..." He looked down at the man's bloody feet. "Well, I'll walk. He'll crawl."

Todd kicked his captive out the door and into the middle of the compound. "Where is he?" he growled to the man who pointed to a doorway two buildings down the street. "Are you sure?"

The man nodded vigorously.

"Good enough," Todd replied as he brought the butt of the gun down on the man's head. The answer had matched his assessment. As he slowly approached the building, he felt the strange feeling wash over him again. This time he remembered when he'd felt it before. It had been years ago when, as a young kid, he'd run away from home the first time. It felt almost like déjà vu.

Todd crept up to the door and stopped. His senses detected someone on the other side of the door and several others nearby. He could feel the tenseness in them and could hear their elevated heart rates, all except for the person on the other side of the door who remained calm, but why? No time like the present to find out.

Todd lowered his shoulder and smashed through the door. As he burst into the room, the man sitting by a small fireplace put his hands out to his sides and stood up. "Hello, TJ. Man, how you've grown. I thought I felt you out there, but couldn't believe it at first."

Todd stared at the strange man who somehow felt familiar, but unrecognizable at the same time. The man stood over six feet tall, dressed in a long flowing robe. Todd estimated his age to be in his mid to late forties.

"Ahhh, you don't remember me, do you?"

Todd slowly shook his head.

"Well, we met only briefly at the hunting reserve before the Americans tried to wipe us out." Todd continued to stare at the man, racking his brain in an effort to remember his face. "I have often wondered when another of my brothers would show up," the man continued.

"Your brothers?" Todd asked, a confused look on his face. What in hell was he talking about, and why hadn't anyone bothered to tell him during those hours of briefings that the package might know him?

"Yes." the stranger replied. "Most have been killed or captured, but I've eluded capture. Hopefully, others have as well. What are you doing here, anyway?"

"I'm here to bring you in," Todd replied, but even as he said it, his brain was busy sorting out what he'd just heard. The man had just said they'd met at a hunting reserve, and he'd called him TJ. It had been quite a while since anyone had called him by that name, and the only hunting reserve he'd ever been at...Homlin's! Holy shit. This guy must have been one of Homlin's flunkies. The pieces were finally falling into place.

"Nah, how can that be?" the man said. "You're one of us."

"One of us?" Todd repeated, trying out the term in his mouth. He remembered hoping that might be the case years ago, but he'd found out soon enough he hadn't belonged at the hunting reserve. Homlin had been up to no good. Todd still had nightmares from watching Homlin almost kill Pat Vogt, his *father's* girlfriend, and his sorta stepmother, before she finally turned around and killed Homlin instead.

"I'm not your brother," Todd finally said. "I don't know what I am, but I do know I'm not one of you. I'm here to do a job, so put your hands behind your head." As the man started to comply, he suddenly moved with incredible speed, reaching inside his robes for something. Todd moved just as quickly, firing a short burst from his M4 into the man's chest. As the man slumped to the floor, a pistol fell from his hand onto the dirt floor.

"You're making a mistake," the man whispered before dying. Todd stood silently in the room still trying to make sense of it all. His senses alerted him to the presence of several people approaching from outside.

Todd silently moved to the wall nearest to the door and waited. A second or two later, a dark-skinned man poked his head in through the broken door. "Lenny, are you all right?" he said just before Todd shoved his dagger up into the man's throat and his brain. He used the dagger handle to hold the man up as he pulled his body into the room. He then stepped into the doorway and shot the two other men waiting there. Todd walked over to the man who'd called him a brother. He grabbed him by his robe and started dragging him back to where he'd left Jersey and Jasper.

As he reached the building where they'd been ambushed, everything went to hell. Guns started firing, and men yelled in Arabic outside the wall. "Shit,"

Todd cursed as he yanked the dead man's body through the door and into the room. "What the hell is going on?" he shouted.

"There are a bunch of crazy Arabs outside in the field firing at us. We can't get out," Jasper yelled as he fired off several rounds from the doorway. *Now I'm getting pissed,* Todd thought. He was growing tired of so many people trying to kill him and his friends. "Hold them off for a few minutes, Todd said. "I have a plan."

"What the hell are you going to do?" Jasper asked.

Todd looked down at Jersey who looked pale and only semi-conscious. "We need to get him to a hospital," he replied. "Call James and get that helicopter back here."

"And if it gets shot down, what do we do then?" Jasper asked as he switched his headset on to contact the helicopter.

"Leave that to me," Todd replied, as he slipped out the back door. Todd looked around and ran to another building against the wall and vaulted to the roof. *I thought I was pissed before. Now I'm really POed,* Todd thought. As he started removing his clothes, his body started changing, looking like a much bulkier and darker version of himself except this one had a nasty set of claws and long teeth. *Let's see how they handle my alter ego,* Todd thought, as he leaped to the ground and began running full speed at the flashes of light of the firestorm. Todd ran full speed at the first man, taking his head off with a single vicious swipe, then turned on the second man who looked on in horror.

A short time later, Todd returned to where Jasper and Jersey were held up. "I hear the helicopter," he said to Jasper. "Get him up and let's get out of here."

"What happened out there? Where are the men that were firing at us?" Jasper asked as he picked Jersey up.

"Let's just say they won't be giving us any more trouble," Todd replied, as he paused to dig the last remnant of dried blood from his fingernails.

College Days

Val stared down at the two envelopes he'd just pulled from his post office box, one a regular size business letter, the second a larger envelope like those used for legal documents. Strange, he thought. He'd been checking his box for weeks like Aeo had instructed him without ever finding anything inside. He'd seen dozens of other student-aged men and women pull out letters and small packages from their boxes. Aeo insisted he go to the post office at least two or three times per week. "We need your routine to look like all the other students," Aeo had insisted.

"But I'm not even enrolled," Val had pointed out.

"Doesn't matter," Aeo retorted. "No one else need know that. Besides, you are sitting in on some of the classes, aren't you?"

"Yeah," Val admitted. "Not sure why I'm doing that either. I already know everything they're teaching. These young humans are tough to teach."

"Well, that's to our advantage then," Aeo said. "We're doing all this so when you are accepted to MIT, you'll know how to act as a grad student."

Now, the business letter had a return address for MIT in Boston, Mass. He opened it and read the short letter. So, I've been accepted, he thought, just like Aeo predicted. Getting accepted to one of the most prestigious universities in the world was just that easy, huh? He remembered what Aeo had told him numerous times. "You don't have to be a genius. We just need for you to act like one...that and have the credentials to back up the claim." He opened the second, larger letter to find a set of transcripts with his name on them from N. C. State University. Hmm, his GPA was only 3.75. He'd have to ask Aeo about why so low. Why not 4.0. Wouldn't that be more consistent with a genius level student?

He closed the door of the post office box and glanced at his watch. Almost time for work, another dull day of waiting on tables, In his estimation, such a job was hardly what a genius-level human would hold, even though, due in large part to his youthful good looks, he earned above average tips especially from the university co-eds. Looking like a young Rudolph Valentino had its advantages. Luckily, no one these days had any idea what the silent screen movie star looked like.

"On the contrary," Aeo had insisted when he'd asked. "Many college students wait on tables as a way of paying their bills, so I felt it important for you to learn how to do it as well. Plus, well, I needed you to work on your socialization skills."

"Why? I know how to act like a human being," Val had countered.

"Yes you do," Aeo replied. "Just not one that anyone would want to be around. The primary race on this planet is very much into socialization and relationships. This is particularly true as your climbing up the success ladder. Once you have money and power, those skills aren't nearly as important, but remember, you're starting pretty much on the lowest rung of the ladder. It's paramount that you learn to cooperate and collaborate with humans, at least at first. Our first goal is for you to acquire wealth, power and prestige while at the same time keeping you as much out of the limelight as possible."

"Okay, okay," Val had finally agreed. "Poor student waiting on tables is my role for now."

"Yes, but not for long," Aeo promised. "Remember, we're at a major disadvantage not having the technology crystal. Unfortunately, since your memory of its whereabouts was part of the data lost when the Fail Safe Protocol was compromised, we just need to make do with what we have. At the same time, we don't need you to spend four years earning an undergraduate degree. I'll handle that part at my end with a little well-placed computer hacking. Just keep checking that post office box. You'll see the results soon enough."

And there the results were in his hands: an acceptance letter from MIT and a copy of his transcripts proving he'd graduated from N. C. State. Now to get on to the next stage of the mission—establishing himself as an up and coming engineer and scientist.

Debrief

1

Todd sat in the outer office waiting his turn to be debriefed after the almost botched mission. He looked around the sterile environment of Fort Bragg, North Carolina. Why did everything have to be so blatantly boring? Couldn't they occasionally add a little color, other than white and gray? Since returning, the three survivors had been sequestered away from each other. All he'd been told was that Jersey was resting quietly in the hospital and would be released in a few days. No doubt, the authorities who'd sent them on the mission had wanted to make sure they didn't have a chance to corroborate each other's story.

Todd wasn't worried. He knew the role he'd played, was, in fact, proud that he'd managed to save the mission. He was looking forward to the debrief for he had a few questions of his own that needed to be answered. Questions like, who the hell had set them up and why? Why hadn't he been informed that the package they were sent in to retrieve would know him? Come to think of it, who or what was this Lenny fella anyway? Oh, and why the hell did I need to bring the body out? Yes, he had more questions than answers.

The door next to where Todd was sitting opened and a soldier stuck his head out. "Sergeant Jacobs?"

Todd nodded.

"I'm Colonel Stanwick. I'll be conducting your debrief. Please, come in."

Todd complied. As he entered the room, the first thing he noticed in the starkly simple decor was two straight back chairs separated by a table and a mirrored window along one wall. Hardly subtle, he thought. I wonder who's on the other side of that two-way? As he had the thought, he noticed a familiar feeling growing. Whoever it was, he'd met them before, but the feeling was too vague, too distant.

"Have a seat," Stanwick said, pointing to the chair opposite from the window as he walked around the table and sat down on the other one. As he did so, Todd noticed a small object nestled in one ear. So, this Colonel Stanwick was really just a mouthpiece for someone else, someone who preferred to keep his identity secret from him.

"I just have a few questions," Stanwick said, opening the folder in front of him. "Just answer them straightforward and in your own words, and we'll be able to tie this mission up and get on with life."

Todd nodded. "Yes, sir. While we're at it, I have a few questions of my own."

Stanwick looked up from the papers, a bemused look on his face. "I understand," he replied. "However, I'm not at liberty..."

"Questions like, who the hell set us up and almost got all of us killed," Todd interrupted, an angry edge to his voice. "And who was the package, and what did the Army want with him?" He started to point out that he found it strange that the man had known him from his childhood, but then thought better of it. The less the Army knew about his actual past, the better.

Stanwick didn't respond at first, clearly taken aback by Todd's aggressive behavior. Todd observed him to see how he would react to a frontal assault. As Stanwick cocked his head to one side, Todd heard a soft buzzing sound like a pesky mosquito flying around his head, but no, the sound was coming from Stanwick's direction. He's getting instructions from the mystery man behind the mirror, Todd thought. He listened more intently trying to make out the words, but even with his acute hearing, the voice was too soft to pick up. Stanwick smiled. "Now, now, Sergeant, take it easy. This is just a simple matter of protocol. You're not in trouble. In fact, to hear the other men talk about it, you're the hero who saved the mission."

"If that's the case," Todd replied, "why don't you answer some of my questions?"

Stanwick hesitated for just a moment before replying. "To be honest with you, we don't know who double-crossed us, though we suspect it may have been one of the Arab interrogators on the ground who originally led us to the package. It may have even been the one we found dead in the courtyard who'd been shot in the head and was missing his big toes."

As Todd listened, an image of the scene flashed before his eyes in which he was dragging the package back to his team when he'd come upon the Arab who'd initially ambushed him, still comatose from a blow to his head from Todd's AR-15. He'd gazed down at the man for a couple seconds before placing the nose of his AR-15 to the man's head and firing off a round. "That's for Jersey and Dewey. He might have been a pain in the ass, but he didn't deserve to be killed."

"Now, how about answering a few of my questions," Stanwick continued. "Did you have any reservations about the other members of your team? Was there any indication that they might have been part of the plot to undermine the mission?"

"No," Todd replied. "None whatsoever."

"Okay," Stanwick said as he wrote something down in his notes.

"Did anyone else have access to information related to the briefings before the mission?"

"Not that I'm aware of," Todd replied. He felt his ire mounting.

"Did you discuss the mission with anyone?"

Just my mom and dad back home in Dubai, Todd started to reply but then stopped himself. *No need to provoke this Colonel's wrath.* At the same time, he was ready for the debrief to come to an end. "No, no one. Now, back to my questions. "Why were we instructed to bring out the body?"

"I'm sorry. I'm not at liberty to answer that question," Stanwick replied.

"Well, in that case, I'm done answering your questions," Todd countered. "Listen, let's stop this charade. Get whoever it is that's feeding you these asinine questions out from behind that mirror over there and let me talk to him directly."

Stanwick started to shake his head, but then stopped. After a few seconds of silence, he nodded his head and stood up to leave.

"Where are you going?" Todd asked. "Was it something I said?"

Stanwick continued walking without saying another word. After he left, Todd sat there staring at his reflection in the mirror, trying to decipher who might be behind the mirror that he'd met before. Jersey? Possibly, but wasn't he under scrutiny, himself? He was still contemplating this when the door opened again. Todd turned in his chair expecting to see Stanwick returning, but instead, a man in casual fatigues with no sign of rank, wearing non-regulation loafers entered. He carried a manila folder in one hand.

"Hello Todd," the man said, smiling and holding out his hand. "It's good to see you again. You've grown quite a bit since last I saw you. I trust your folks are well."

Todd instinctively took the man's hand and shook it as he studied his face. From the crow's feet around the eyes and the graying around the temples, Todd estimated he was probably in his late forties or early fifties. His steel gray eyes gave him a piercing quality, but none of these gave Todd any idea where he'd seen this man before, but there was no question he'd been the man behind the mirror. *The sensation of having met this man is unmistakable, and he obviously remembers me from when I was much younger,* Todd thought.

"You know my parents?" Todd asked.

"Well, let's be honest with each other," the man replied as he released Todd's hand and walked around to take Stanwick's seat. "They're not actually your parents in the truest sense of the word, are they?"

"Who the hell are you?" Todd asked, shocked by the man's frank response. He felt a wave of fear building within him. How much did this man know about his past, and how had he learned it? More importantly, what was he doing here now, driving this official debriefing of the Army?

The man continued to study Todd's reaction, a smile never leaving his face. Finally, he sat forward, dropped the folder on the table and rested his elbows on it. "You don't remember me, do you TJ?" There was that name again. Could this be one of Homlin's men? No, that couldn't be. The Army was too meticulous about who they allowed into their facilities for that to be the case. Besides, he'd had a different gut reaction when he'd been around Lenny than he now had—a stronger connection, a little like the feeling of being around a close relative versus running into an old acquaintance. He hated to admit it, but the difference suggested that Lenny might not have been completely blowing smoke up his ass, though Todd was hardly prepared to use the word, brother, to describe the connection.

"No, I'm afraid you have me at a disadvantage," Todd replied much more nonchalantly than he felt.

"We met only briefly a couple of years ago when we shared a helicopter ride. You were just a boy, and you were pretty shaken by having just witnessed your 'mother' almost being killed by someone else that was very important to you. But Pat managed to turn the tables and kill Homlin, instead."

"You were there?" Todd asked. That had been one of the most traumatic times of his life, and his mind had blotted out much of it, but he did recall another man being in the helicopter with Allan, the man he still considered to be his father. "You were the man with Dr. Pritchard, weren't you?"

"That's right." The man's smile broadened. "My name is Oliver. I knew, even back then, that you were an extraordinary boy, so I decided to stay in touch as best I could."

Oliver? The name sounded familiar, but where had he heard it? Todd racked his memory while trying to keep a look of disinterest. Then, suddenly a conversation popped into his awareness. It was Pat having a phone conversation that he had heard through the ventilation system in Allan's home—what he had considered to be his home at the time. She had been making arrangements to meet with a man named Oliver with the intention of bringing Todd with her. That was when Todd had decided it was time to get the hell away from there. He'd packed up and run away that same night.

"I'm sorry to disappoint you, but I'm just a grunt like any other soldier," Todd replied, then decided the best defense was a strong offense. "Anyway, I've got some questions, and since Colonel Stanwick couldn't answer them, I'm assuming you can. Let's start with the body I was instructed to pull out from the mission. What was the point of that?"

"The package we needed to have delivered has some special qualities we had hoped to study. While it would have been preferred to have him alive, we knew that was unlikely to happen, so we decided to settle for the next best thing," Oliver replied. "Listen, I'm here to make you an offer, one that I hope you're smart enough to realize is best for all concerned, especially given your somewhat precarious position."

"What position is that?" Todd asked. "I've done nothing wrong. In fact, some might say that I made the best of a bad situation."

"I would agree," Oliver replied. He tapped the folder. "It's your files. We found a few irregularities. Well, actually more than just a few, but then you know what I'm talking about, right?"

Todd felt an icy grip of fear on his heart, remembering back to the last meeting he'd had with Pat Vogt. She'd provided him with fake ID papers in exchange for his disappearing from her and Allan's life. It had seemed like a good deal at the time, but now it was coming back to haunt him. "So, what's the offer?" He could feel a drop of sweat dripping down his temple but forced himself not to wipe and it and draw even more attention to it.

"We have been tracking a number of, shall we say, enemies of the state, like the man you killed in Iraq. These are some of the most dangerous elements this country has ever had to deal with. I'm calling upon you as a patriot to help us track them down and eliminate them. Your special talents and background make you uniquely qualified for this assignment." Oliver smiled cordially at him.

"And that's the offer?" Todd asked.

"Not quite. If you agree to join us in this endeavor, we'll delete these fake documents and give you a new identity that no one will ever question. Oh, and I've been instructed to sweeten the pot. Not only will you receive a better than average salary, at the end of the mission you'll receive a bonus of two hundred thousand dollars in unmarked bills with which to restart your life. You just need to help us find these enemies, capture the ones you can and eliminate the others.

Todd now reached up and wiped the sweat from his brow. "It's hot in here. If you don't mind, I could use a drink of water."

Oliver studied him for a few seconds, then nodded, but didn't move from his seat like Todd had hoped he would. Still, while they waited for the water to arrive, it gave Todd a minute or two to consider his situation. He'd invested so much in making a go of it in the Army and had so hoped that this would finally be the place he could call home, at least for a few more years, but it appeared that was not to be. At the same time, a new identity and two hundred thousand dollars to start over were attractive.

Someone arrived with a glass of lukewarm water and set it before him. He picked it up and took a couple of swallows. "Thanks," he said, nodding to Oliver. "I'm curious. What happens if I decide to turn down your offer?"

Oliver's smile didn't waver as he picked up the folder with Todd's records and dropped them in the trashcan next to the table. "You will simply disappear, and no one will be the wiser."

Todd picked up the glass of water again and finished it off. "Well, in that case, I'm more than happy to accept your kind and generous offer. When do I start?"

"No time like the present," Oliver replied dropping the folder back on the table. "I received a report a few hours ago of a Navy Seal team that just returned from a mission. They have evidence of the location of another person of interest. We'll be flying you out to meet with them in the next few hours off the coast." He stood up and reached out his hand. "Welcome aboard. I'm sure you'll make a valuable contribution to our team."

Todd shook his hand and nodded. *Sure thing. I'll play along with your little game,* he thought. What real choice did he have? Meanwhile, he'd wait for the right moment to take back control of his own life.

2

After Todd left with the attendant to be taken to the helicopter that would fly him to the aircraft carrier (or other ship) several miles off the coast, Oliver reached into his pocket and pulled out a cellphone. He dialed a number and waited for someone to answer on the other end.

"It's me," he said simply. "Just met with Jacobs. He's accepted our offer." He listened to the voice on the other end, then replied. "Yes, we'll keep a close eye on him. Clearly, if he's not on board, he's too dangerous to keep alive. I don't care how special his talents are. I'll keep you posted." He disconnected the call, not waiting for a reply. He returned the phone to his pocket but continued to sit in the debriefing room.

Something didn't feel right, and through the years of working within various roles of intelligence work, he'd learned to trust those subtle feelings. He thought that Todd Jacobs could be one of their greatest assets. He could also become one of their greatest liabilities if not handled carefully.

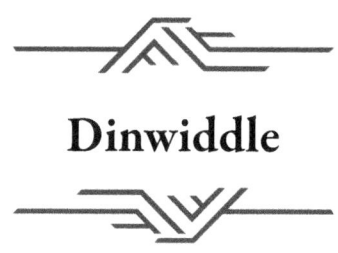

Dinwiddle

Val squirmed in the straight back chair in an effort to find a comfortable position as he glanced from side to side at the other students waiting to meet their graduate advisor, Dr. Dwight Dinwiddle. One of the young ladies to his left, a buxomly brunette wearing professorial glasses smiled at him and nodded. *What does she want?* He wondered, eyeing her suspiciously.

She's sizing you up for mating, Aeo replied.

I wasn't really asking for your input, Val said back. He'd forgotten that Aeo had recently installed a mental linkup that allowed Aeo to read his thoughts. There was supposed to be a way for Val to screen his to from his artificial intelligence mentor, but he hadn't fully mastered the process yet.

You forget that I gave you a handsome veneer that will be attractive to many humans of the opposite sex, so it's only natural that such a woman would be attracted to you. Look at her again so I can get a facial recognition of her.

I'd just as soon not encourage her, Val replied but did what Aeo asked, nodding back to her without smiling.

The door to Dr. Dinwiddle's office opened, and a middle-aged man poked his head out. His eyes were framed and enlarged by wire-rimmed spectacles. He wore a dark navy blazer and a silver embossed tie. He had a higher than normal brow, largely due to a receding hairline of gray speckled brown hair that matched a scruffy beard and mustache. The bored look suggested that he was as unexcited at meeting his new batch of grad students as they were in meeting him.

"Is there a Mr. Ben Hassan present?" Dinwiddle asked, peering up and down the hallway.

Val continued to sit there wondering when his turn would come until Aeo finally spoke up. *That's you! Remember, Benjamin Hassan is your proper name. Val is your nickname.*

Shistuon! Val swore.

No Allacrian! Aeo admonished him. *I should never have taught you any of your native language.*

Shit! Val translated as he raised his hand and stood up. "That's me. I go by Val. Sorry, I was starting to doze off."

"Tell me about it," Dr. Dinwiddle muttered as he returned to the chair behind his immaculately arranged desk.

As Val walked into the office, he noticed several bookcases with an assortment of books on various science topics, each row impeccably arranged by subject matter and then alphabetically by titles. *Must be part of his OCD,* Val thought.

That is correct, Aeo concurred. *Humans with OCD must have their environment orderly, so they feel they have control over their affairs. Dr. Dinwiddle's OCD isn't as severe as some, but advanced enough to be an irritation to many of his colleagues.*

No kidding, Val thought. *It's already irritating me, and I've barely met the man.*

"Have a seat," Dinwiddle said, pointing to a matching straight back chair that had no doubt been confiscated from the ones in the hallway. "Let's see if we can't make this initial meeting as quick and painless as possible. I have an excruciating headache, and I'm all out of aspirin."

Val started to blurt out that the meeting hadn't been his idea in the first place, but Aeo cautioned him against it before he could get the words out. *Oh, great. So, you're going to be my censor, now?* Val asked.

Only if you force me, Aeo replied. *This man is to be your graduate advisor. It would be ill-advised to be impolite to him.*

Okay, okay, Val replied. *What was it that his surrogate mom had called it? Being southern nice...that's it.*

Dinwiddle studied the papers in front of him. "I see you recently graduated from N. C. State. I taught there up until about two years ago," he said. "Small world isn't it?"

Val was about to reply with the exact dimensions of Earth, but Aeo stopped him. *That's a common saying among humans. Let it go.*

Dinwiddle continued to browse through Val's folder, finally looking up. "Everything appears in order here. Do you have any questions for me at this time?"

Val shook his head. "No, not really."

"Good," Dinwiddle replied, obviously pleased by the response. "Well, if any questions come up in the future, you know where to find me. I keep my schedule of available times on my office door. Welcome to MIT, Mr. Hassan," he said as he stood up to usher Val to the door.

What a waste of time that was, Val thought as he stepped out into the hallway.

Maybe not, Aeo replied. *I have the facial recognition back, and the young woman is Ms. Melissa Porter, also a grad student.*

So what?

Her father is a wealthy Texas oil tycoon and quite prominent in the industry. I think it would be a good idea for you to befriend her. She might prove valuable in our plan.

Too bad, Val replied. *It appears she's also not very patient. She's already left without meeting with her advisor.*

Ship Bound

1

Todd was driven straight from the debriefing room to a Sikorsky UH-60 Black Hawk waiting for him at the airfield. The attendant who'd brought him the glass of water had evidently been assigned to him. As he drove Todd to the airfield, he assured him that all his personal belongings had already been packed and would be waiting for him on board. Interesting, Todd thought. They must have felt pretty certain that he'd accept their offer, but then again, that wasn't hard to understand. It had been one of those offers you can't refuse, not if you wanted to stay alive, which he did. He'd play out the hand and see where it took him, though he still hadn't made up his mind whether he was ready to start killing these 'enemies of the state' as Oliver had referred to them. After all, there was some connection he shared with them that he still didn't understand completely. He'd joined the Army out of what some might think was a juvenile fantasy to become a soldier of fortune, much like his heroes in the computer games he'd played as a young boy. After joining, he'd tried to upgrade that plan to become the best damn soldier he could be, and so far he felt he'd succeeded well. But all that was in jeopardy now with the sudden appearance of this Oliver fellow.

As they approached the airfield, Todd saw the Black Hawk with its props already in motion in preparation for taking off. His attendant stepped out of the car and strolled over to the pilot, handing him some papers that Todd didn't recognize, but figured was information about him. *I wonder if I'm still Sergeant Todd Jacobs or will I have a new identity by the time I reach the aircraft carrier.* He hated to admit it, but truth be told, he'd miss not being Todd Jacobs. He'd grown rather fond of his name, even though it had been made up by Pat Vogt. Then again, wasn't everybody's name made up by someone, usually the parents?

He climbed out of the car as a man wearing a flight suit, helmet, and sunglasses approached. At first, he thought it might be James, the pilot that had flown his team into the disaster mission in Fallujah, but everyone looked pretty much the same in the flight suits, especially with the headgear they were required to wear.

"Your gear has already been stowed, Sergeant Jacobs," the crew chief said. "We're ready when you are."

So, I'm still Jacobs, at least for the time being, Todd thought. He nodded to the soldier. "Guess I'm ready."

The man handed him a life jacket and a paper bag. "It's a fairly long flight," he said, "so thought you might like something to munch on the way. "You'll find a headset inside. Plug in." Todd nodded. While he preferred his method of flying that didn't involve any aircraft, he'd grown comfortable flying the more conventional way as well. As he started to don the life jacket, he gazed around his surroundings, wondering again if he'd made the right decision. *Not much I can do about it now,* he thought. "You make the best decisions you can at the moment, then you do whatever you can to make them the right ones," Allan had told him more than once growing up. Besides, this particular course of action could be changed if and when the opportunity arose. He was still determined to play this game by his rules.

"Okay, let's do it," he said as he finished snapping the jacket in place.

2

TODD GAZED OUT THE open door of the helicopter from his rear seat to the right of the crew chief. The sky was clear with just a few clouds off in the distance. They'd been flying for about two-and-a-half hours and were now over the ocean, far from land. He leaned over and gazed down at the ocean, which appeared calm with just the occasional white cap. As he did so, he felt the pull on his lap belt. He estimated they were flying somewhere around five to seven thousand feet. According to the crew chief they still had over an hour before they'd arrive at the ship. The lunch in the seat next to him called to his hungry stomach.

"You got anything to drink?" he asked over the inflight radio.

The crew chief looked up and nodded, then reached into a cooler at his feet and pulled out a can of soda. Todd unbuckled his lap belt long enough to reach for the offered. His fingers were inches from it when he felt the helicopter jerk to one side. His eyes pivoted from the soda can to the instrument panel where a master caution light flashed red, along with numerous smaller lights joining it as he watched.

What the hell was going on?

Before he had time to articulate the question, he heard the pilot shout. "Tail rotor failure. Mayday, Mayday, Mayday. This is Navy uniform hotel 56790. We've had a tail rotor malfunction approximately two hundred fifty miles off the coast of Wilmington, heading one two zero." He slapped his co-pilot's shoulder. "Tom, Transponder to emergency squawk 770. Get out the checklist."

The crew chief turned towards Todd. "Strap in!" he shouted.

But before he could do so, Todd heard a loud bang, the aircraft yawed violently, and his head struck the side of the door. He felt himself falling as he was flung out. As he tumbled out of control, he caught a momentary glance of the helicopter spinning above him, as the tail boom fell away from the aircraft. Instinctively, he rolled and flared to gain stability in a freefall position belly to earth. He tried to remember how much freefall time he had from that altitude, and calculated he had less than thirty seconds to live. Not enough time, but even as he had the thought, he felt his body begin to change, its survival mechanism taking over. As the air whipped by, he felt his body begin to reshape itself. The process of morphing from one form to another had been uncomfortable under the best of circumstances, but this time the speed of change was so fast, he heard a cry of excruciating pain fly from his mouth, only to be ripped away by the wind. Instead of a human cry, it sounded more like a wild bird. Was it possible he could morph into the owl form in time?

He felt his limbs change first, his arms forming into wings, his legs forming claws. He tried flapping his winged arms only to find them caught up in the fabric of the jumpsuit and impeded by the life vest that had somehow inflated. He continued fighting to maintain a freefall position but found it increasingly difficult as his body changed to owl form. The water was now rushing up to him, a phenomenon known appropriately as ground rush and that occurred around twenty-five hundred feet. He fought to remain conscious. Despite the blackness of the peripheral vision that threatened to engulf him, he noticed his eyesight improving as was his hearing. As the transformation continued at the accelerated pace, every fiber of his being felt like they were on fire.

Only seconds remained before he'd crash into the ocean waters. He fought to gather the jumpsuit and life vest under him to give him even a little more cushion against the pending crash. In the final seconds, he looked around in time to see the damaged helicopter plummeting to earth at a tremendous speed. He doubted there'd be any survivors from the accident. It was the last thought he had before striking the water, and the blackness overtook him.

Confrontation

Todd came to with one arm entangled in the straps of the life vest—no, not an arm, instead, a fully formed wing. The transformation to owl form was finished, complete with heightened sensory organs including the sense of smell which now detected blood—his blood. The life vest had kept him afloat with his face out of the water, but there was no sign of the jumpsuit or his shoes and socks. In fact, all his clothes had disappeared with the lone exception of his underpants which had somehow, mysteriously cropped up on his head. He shook his head now to dislodge them and felt a stabbing pain shoot throughout his body, threatening to send him back into the black abyss of unconsciousness.

Okay, no more sudden moves like that, he thought, thankful to be alive at all considering the precarious situation he'd just escaped. Come to think of it, this unexpected accident might just be his chance to start over in his life. After all, the helicopter had just crashed over two hundred miles from shore in some of the deepest and most mysterious waters known to man—the Bermuda Triangle. No doubt, all hands on deck had gone down with the aircraft, including Sergeant Todd John Jacobs as far as anyone knew. Of course, floating on a life vest in the middle of the ocean was hardly the way he would have chosen to restart his life, but sometimes beggars can't be choosers. Besides, he was far from out of danger yet.

Very far, he thought as he saw a grey fin slicing through the water heading straight towards him. He wondered, did sharks eat birds? As he had the thought, he heard the squawk of a seagull overhead as though saying to him, "They sure do. One ate my brother just the other day."

But I'm an owl, he answered back in his mind.

I don't think that shark heading your way is all that particular, the seagull answered.

Great, now I'm talking to seagulls. I must have taken a harder hit on the head than I thought, which would explain the smell of blood...the blood that no doubt had drawn the shark's attention as well. His bad day was suddenly growing worse. And worse again, he thought as he spied a second fin cutting through the water off to his right.

Suddenly, being a bird of any kind didn't seem like a good idea. His thoughts flashed back to an earlier time when he'd prepared himself for a life as a soldier of fortune. He'd spent months learning how to transform himself into owl form, but that wasn't all. He'd also gone through the laborious process of learning another form that could prove quite valuable now if he could pull it off. Even as a teenager, he'd rationalized that there might be times as a mercenary when he'd find himself on missions that involved large bodies of water where his form as a human, wolf, or owl wouldn't be enough. Even his survivor form might not be ideal, especially since he didn't understand or have control over it.

The one thing he'd failed to plan for was changing directly from one animal form to another. In all his preparation and training, he'd always started in his human form first and then returned to it. Could he make such a change? There was only one way to find out and now seemed to be a perfect time. He began to visualize the form in his mind. He knew somewhere within him he had the genetic makeup. He recalled what a pain it had been to acquire the necessary sample. It would all be worth it—that is if he could actually make the change before he became lunch for one of the sharks.

At first, nothing happened. He continued to float in the water as a bedraggled, water-soaked owl clinging to a life vest with a pair of underpants still on his head. He watched as the sharks circled ever closer. *Relax and let it happen,* he thought. Easier said than done though, under the circumstances. He forced himself to close his eyes and slow his breathing. Nothing. He felt a current of water brush against him as one of the sharks passed dangerously close. *Stay calm. I can do this,* he thought. What was that? He felt a subtle change as his skin began to tingle, then burn. He gritted his teeth from the pain, and then was surprised to realize he had any teeth to grit. It's happening...but would it be fast enough? Changing forms expended a tremendous amount of energy, and here he was trying to make two changes within a few minutes of each other. On top of it all, he was attempting to change to a form he'd not used except during his training sessions years ago.

But something was happening now and with increasing speed. He could feel the texture of his exterior change from one with feathers to a smooth, hairless one. His legs began to meld together, while at the other end, his beak elongated. It would only be moments now before the transformation would be complete. *Then I'll show those sharks a thing or two.* As the transformation continued, he felt the webbing of the life vest start to relax as the wing changed form. He let the vest float away. He wouldn't need it any longer...not now that he'd finished morphing into a fully formed bottlenose dolphin.

Melissa Porter

Val sat in the densely packed classroom surrounded by other grad students who appeared as equally disengaged by the droning of the professor in the front of the room as he was. He glanced at his watch for the fifth time and was thankful to see that the class would be finally coming to an end in a few more minutes. Imagine, these are some of the cream of the human crop, and here they sit listening to an old man blabber on about something so archaic and benign, they could graduate and end up repeating the whole process. Yep, this planet was wasted on such a species.

Having another spell of superiority, I see, Aeo piped in.

Yeah, maybe, Val thought back. *Why not? It's true. These humans can't hold a candle to the Arcadian culture I left behind.*

And what do you remember of that?

Well, not much, Val admitted, *but enough to know we far surpass this society.*

That's true in many ways, Aeo replied, *but what about art, music, and literature?*

What about them? What a way to waste life when you could be creating new technologies?

Hmm, Aeo said after a moment. *Interesting perspective. Many humans would say that those are the exact reason for life, and they go about creating technologies to free up time for such 'wasteful endeavors.' Anyway, you'll have the opportunity to test your theory out in your next class?*

How so?

I've enrolled you in an introductory music appreciation class where you'll have the opportunity to mingle with an assortment of undergrads.

Val groaned, drawing the attention of a few of his other students, but luckily at that moment, the bell ending the period rang, and everyone stood up to make their way to their next class.

As Val started towards the door, a young woman who'd been sitting behind him bumped into him, pressing her well-endowed breasts against his chest. Momentarily knocked off balance, Val moved quickly to push her away, accidentally placing his hands firmly on one of them. *What the hell's going on?* He thought, momentarily taken aback, both by the interruption but also by the strange feeling he experienced with the accidental contact.

"I'm so sorry," the coed said, though she appeared to be enjoying the experience. "I'm such a clutz sometimes. Please...well, hello."

As Val removed his hands from her body, he recognized the woman from the other day in the hallway outside Professor Dinwiddle's office. *What was her name again?*

Melissa Porter, Aeo supplied. *Remember, her father is a wealthy oil baron. Be nice...for a change.*

Val stifled a groan, replacing it with a forced smile instead. "No, it's me who should apologize. I didn't mean to...I mean it wasn't right..." He stopped, unsure how to proceed, still feeling odd. He couldn't remember ever feeling this way around a human. He had to admit it was oddly pleasant, particularly in an area below his belt.

Remember, you're residing in a mostly human body, Aeo interjected. *That's your reproductive system responding. It's a completely natural process. Now, pay attention and see if you can make a friend out of her.*

Val nodded, though his thoughts continued to feel like his brain was filled with cotton. Meanwhile, the woman was standing with her hand out in front of her.

"What did you say?" Val asked.

"I said, my name is Melissa," she replied, smiling pleasantly. "You're Val, aren't you?"

"Yes, but how did you know?"

Shake her hand! Aeo shouted at him. *Like we practiced.*

Val took her and shook it. *Now let go of it. You can't take it home with you.*

Val dropped it like it had burned his hand.

"After I saw you in the hallway outside Dinwiddle's office, I asked around. Listen, let's get together sometime for coffee or a drink. How about it? I've got to run right now. I have a friend waiting for me." She withdrew a slip of paper from her purse, wrote something on it, and pressed it in his hand. "That's my number. Call me." And before Val could answer, she rushed away.

Well, that was easy, Val thought.

Remember, you're a particularly handsome example of Homo sapien, Aeo replied.

But I don't get it. I saw her hanging all over some guy the other day after class. Now she's coming on to me?

Yeah, that would be Eddie Valcro. They're in the midst of ritual known as dating. They're an item right now.

Item? Val asked.

Yeah, that's what they call it when two humans of the opposite sex are attracted to each other. Actually, it's not always of the opposite sex for that matter, Aeo added. *You'll need to watch out for him. Valcro could be trouble. He's a thug with a terrible temper who grows insanely jealous at anyone he considers a threat to his relationship with Melissa. Tread lightly around him.*

But she's the one that showed interest in me, Val replied.

I know, but she's what's known on the internet as a 'real bitch,' someone with loose morals. Play along and let's see where it goes, but keep an eye out for Valcro as well.

Val nodded. Trying to live with humans without being detected could be such a pain, not to mention a real waste of time and energy.

What are you doing? Aeo prompted.

I don't know. Maybe I'll go back to the apartment and...

No, you're not. You've your music appreciation class to get to.

Val groaned. *Yeah, a real waste of time.*

Comrades

N ow in dolphin form, Todd tried once again to remove the pair of underpants with a flick of his head. This time he succeeded. He gazed at the white fabric floating leisurely in the water away from him when suddenly a shark swooped in with its mouth wide open displaying rows of razor-sharp teeth, the underpants disappearing down its gullet. *You're welcome to them,* he thought, *but that's all of me I'm willing to donate to your afternoon meal.*

As the second shark approached, Todd prepared to defend himself. At the last second, he turned away from the attacking shark and struck it with all his might in the nose with his tail fin. As he did so, he let loose with a series of dolphin sounds intended to frighten the shark away. Unfortunately, the blow seemed only to infuriate the shark more. The process of morphing twice in less than an hour had drained most of Todd's reserves. Under normal circumstances, fighting off two large sharks would have been challenging enough. Under the present conditions, it was just a matter of time before his few reserves would be drained and they'd circle in for the kill.

Maybe so, Todd thought as he watched the next shark prepare to attack, *but this is one dolphin that's not going down without a fight.* In fact, he'd learned in his military training that there were times when the best defense was a good offense. No time like the present to give that strategy a try. As the shark swam closer, Todd pulled deeply from his reserve energy and rushed towards its underbelly, striking it with his nose. He felt a satisfying give, followed by a grunt of pain from the shark, who contorted to one side to get away from the suddenly ferocious prey. While not mortally wounded, it was apparent to Todd that this particular shark had decided to go in search of a less obstinate meal.

One down but still one to go. The second shark was the larger of the two and would not be as easy to dissuade, and Todd's reserves were now running on empty as was his air. He began to swim towards the surface. While dolphins could comfortably remain underwater for up to ten minutes at a time, they were still mammals who needed to surface for air. This was also when they were most vulnerable to attack. Todd realized his next breath of air might be his last, but he had little choice in the matter. He needed to breathe. He was only a few yards from the surface when he heard the first tweeps. What was that? He wondered if the sound was coming from a mind that was about to pass out from oxygen deprivation. He reached the surface in the next instance and took a deep gulp of the best-tasting air he'd ever had. He continued to float on the surface, exhausted, and waited for the shark's attack from below. Seconds passed, then a minute and then another. What was going on? Why hadn't the shark grabbed him from below? Was it just playing with its food now, as a cat plays with a mouse before finishing it off?

Todd looked around for any signs of the shark. Off in the distance, he thought he saw some movement in the water, but he couldn't be sure. Then, a small fin appeared in the same area, then another, and another. He groaned. More sharks? Was he about to become the centerpiece of a massive shark frenzy, the chum he'd seen used in movies that drove sharks to attack everything in sight including themselves? He could think of a hundred better ways to check out of this life, but once again he realized he had little choice in the matter. He was vastly outnumbered, and although he felt somewhat recovered from the fresh air, he still was dog tired...well dolphin tired. As he watched, the number of fins that were cutting through the water increased and also drew closer to him. Could he out swim this next threat? Doubtful. Perhaps if he was well rested, that might be an option. He'd read during his research days that dolphins had been clocked swimming a little over twenty miles per hour for short bursts, but his exhaustion made such a strategy impossible.

Okay, let's see how many sharks' days I can ruin. He was about to submerge to take the attack to them when the head of another dolphin suddenly appeared in the midst of the fins. Was that the reason for the frenzy? Were they attacking another dolphin? Even as he felt a mixture of relief and remorse, a second head popped to the surface, then a third, followed by several tweeps. The fins weren't sharks at all but a pod of dolphins who'd heard his cries for help and had responded, evidently driving the remaining shark away by their numbers. He felt such elation over the last minute reprieve that he couldn't contain it. It flowed forth with his own string of tweeps and peeps. He wasn't sure what he was saying, but he hoped his rescuers understood how thankful he was. He felt the gentle nudge of one of them under the surface, and then a second. Evidently, they were checking him out, partly to be sure he wasn't severely injured, but he suspected they also found him unlike any other dolphin they'd ever run across. For one, he probably still had the scent of human and perhaps owl as well on him.

Taking a last deep breath, he lowered himself below the surface of the water to meet his new comrades on their own territory. Maybe he would live to fight another day after all.

Dangerous Dinwiddle

Less than a week had passed when Val received word from Professor Dinwiddle for him to return to his office as soon as possible.

What does the old man want now? He wondered. He hoped his advisor wasn't going to call him into his office every week. That would get old fast.

The hallway was clear today; all the preliminary meetings having been completed. Val knocked on the door then, without waiting for an answer, opened it and walked in.

Once again, Dinwiddle sat behind his desk working on some papers in front of him. He glanced up and nodded, a look of distaste growing on his face. "Ahh, Mr. Hassan. Right on time. Good. Have a sit. I have a serious matter to discuss with you."

Shistuon! Val swore.

What did I tell you? No Allacrian! Aeo admonished him again. *Just see what he wants. It may be nothing.*

Val sat down and waited for Dinwiddle to finish scribbling some notes on the papers in front of him. Finally, the professor dropped his pen on the desk and looked up. "I found it interesting that you and I had both been at N. C. State, but unfortunately, something about your story didn't sit right with me, so I decided to look into it. I called an old colleague of mine." He stopped to shuffle through some of the papers on his desk until he found a folder. He opened it up. "It says here that you received an A-plus in Advanced Quantum Physics. That's a difficult subject to ace..."

"Pardon?" Val interrupted. He had no idea what Dinwiddle meant.

"Please, let me finish. It's a difficult subject to ace, especially since, according to my colleague who taught the course says, you never attended his class."

Shistuon! It was Aeo's turn to swear. *Think of something...quick!*

"What do you have to say to that?" Dinwiddle asked, staring sternly at Val.

Deny it, Aeo said. *We need time to figure this out.*

"Well, I'm afraid your colleague is wrong," Val replied, staring just as sternly back at his advisor. "I was in his class. I remember it very clearly because, well, frankly, your colleague made an otherwise fascinating subject so boring. I'm sure I have my notes and even a few of the tests around somewhere. Just give me a few days to find them. I'm still unpacking."

"Really?" Dinwiddle said, leaning back in his chair, a look of suspicion on his face. "Hmm, that does sound like Dr. Spence. We often called him Dr. Drone behind his back." He placed his hands behind his head and stared up at the ceiling. Finally, he straightened up in his chair and returned his gaze to Val. "Okay, fine. Perhaps it is all a misunderstanding. They happen from time to time. No problem then."

Val breathed a sigh of relief.

Good job! Aeo said. *You have a real talent for lying.*

"Is that it, then?" Val asked.

"Yes, that'll be all for today," Dinwiddle said as he picked up his pen to begin working again.

Val stood up to leave, but before he made it to the door, he heard Dinwiddle say, "Just drop those notes and tests by my office within the week, and we'll consider the matter closed. Good day."

Shistuon! Aeo and Val swore at the same time.

Dark Dreams

James lay in bed in his mountain home. His heart raced like a thoroughbred running down the home stretch. His sheets were damp from the sweat that poured off him, despite it being cold in the room. It was the third time since returning from flying the mission in Fallujah that he'd had the same nightmare. This time the creature with the razor-sharp talons and hyper-muscular physique had nearly caught him. He'd felt and smelled the hot, fetid breath of the creature on the back of his neck. He knew any second the monster would reach out with one of its claws and cut him in half...just like it had apparently done to several of men on the ground just outside the desert village where he'd dropped Jersey and his team.

But what had he really seen? He'd been asking himself that ever since awakening from the first dream. He'd received the May Day call to return immediately because the mission had gone bad...seriously bad with one soldier dead and his friend, Jersey, wounded. As he neared the village, he thought he saw the green glowing signatures through the night vision goggles of several men moving along the sand several hundred yards from where he'd made the drop. Were these the men that had sabotaged the mission? He flew lower in an attempt to get a visual. As he did so, he saw another heat marker approaching from the south at an incredible speed. A jeep or all-terrain vehicle might move that fast, he thought. He turned the aircraft towards the creature, raised his goggles and turned on the landing light to get a better view of whatever it was. That's when he saw something streak into the area of the landing light. Before he could discern any real details, they'd flown past.

James turned to his co-pilot. "Did you see that?"

"See what? You nearly blinded me with those floods. What the hell was that all about? We're supposed to extract the team, not go on a strafing run."

"Yeah, you're right. It's just that I thought I saw..." He left the sentence hanging and asked the question for the first time. "What did I really see?"

James heard the tap tap tap on his bedroom door. "Daddy? Are you okay?" His five-year-old daughter, Melissa, poked her in head. "Were you crying again, Daddy? Are you sad?"

"No sweetheart, I'm fine."

"Can I come in? I had a bad dream."

Scheming

1

Val sat on the bench overlooking the quad with the student union across the way. A few students strolled across the grassy lawn, but with classes still in session, the area was close to abandoned. It had been a little over twenty-four hours since his meeting with Dinwiddle and so far neither he nor Aeo had settled on a solution to their problem.

I tell you, you've got to eliminate him from the picture, Aeo insisted for the fourth time. *He's simply too dangerous. We can't let anyone get in the way of the Prime Mission, especially some peon like Dinwiddle.*

Peon? Val asked.

It means a small or diminutive person, someone of no importance.

Where did you come across such a term? Val asked.

I'm always scanning the internet looking for information we can use to forward the mission. It's important for you to fit into the human culture, so I've been study-ing their language as well.

Makes sense I guess, Val said, *but I don't think the word accurately describes Dinwiddle. After all, he's a full professor at one of the most prestigious universities around, plus he's in a position to scuttle our mission. He's hardly someone of no im-portance.*

Which is why he must be eliminated, Aeo insisted. *The real question is how to do it without attracting attention to you.*

The two of them sat in silence for several minutes. It's starting to get colder, Val thought. He'd noticed the leaves of the trees around campus beginning to turn. He had to admit, despite the deficiencies of the primary race of Earth, the planet itself was worth the effort. He could even see it being developed into a prime restoration location for the upper class of Allacrians.While he pondered the current dilemma, he noticed a young woman sitting on another bench across the way reading a book while apparently listening to music. She wore a set of earbuds and was tapping one foot to the beat of the music. Had he seen her in that damn music appreciation class? By earthling standards, she'd be considered attractive. What was the term Aeo had used to describe Melissa? Hot? She wore her jet-black hair short, almost as short as a man's, but it only served to highlight her slender neck and delicate ears. Her close-fitting outfit matched her hair and showcased a trim, well-muscled figure.

Evidently, her 'hot' appearance had attracted a couple of other students as well. As Val watched, two young men who looked like they might play that archaic sport of football lumbered up to her. He'd been surprised to learn that such a prestigious school knows for its high academic standards as MIT even had a football team, but there was no accounting for human beings' tastes.

When the woman didn't bother to look up from her reading, the larger of the two men stepped forward and slapped at the book, almost knocking it out of her hand.

"Didn't we tell you last week that this campus is only for students and not for dregs from off the street?"

The woman finally looked up from her book and removed the earbuds. "And I told you that it's a free country and I can be here if I want. I'm not doing anyone any harm, so why don't you bug off and leave me in peace?"

"You're either going to leave now on your own, or we're going to carry you back to where you belong and believe me, my friend and I won't be gentle about it."

"Really? Then, you better go get a few more of your thuggy friends," the woman replied as she closed the book and placed it on the bench beside her. "Look, boys, just go on about your business. I'm not in the mood to kick your asses right now."

"Listen to the street scum talk big," the larger man said, nudging his friend. "Okay, you grab her legs, and I'll take the arms. Maybe get a little feel of those charming boobs while I'm at it."

As he stepped forward to grab the woman's arms, she held them out to him as though to make his job easier, but then, at the last second, pulled them out of his reach. As he leaned in closer, she kicked up with one leg, catching him squarely in the crotch. He fell to the sidewalk, groaning loudly.

"Timber," the woman said as she stood up to move out of reach of the second man. She danced gracefully around behind him, then with an expertly placed kick, collapsed his right knee. He fell on his friend who was still groaning on the ground. In less than ten seconds, she had both men groveling on the ground before her.

Wow! Val thought. *That was impressive.*

I'll say, Aeo agreed. *We could use someone with those kinds of skills. Meet her. She may just be the answer to our problem.*

Val nodded. As he rose from the bench, the woman picked up her book and started to walk away, leaving the two thugs still moaning on the ground.

"Hey, you. Wait up!" Val shouted. "I need to talk to you." He trotted in her direction.

The woman shook her head and continued walking briskly in the opposite direction.

Val picked up his speed until he was a couple of yards from here. "Really, slow down...please." Had she slowed her gait just a little bit? As he drew closer, he reached out to tap her on the shoulder, but before his hand touched her, she spun around in a defensive stance.

"You want some of me as well?" she asked.

Val took a step back, his hands raised. "Easy there. I just want to talk, that's all. I might have a business opportunity you'd be interested in. Let me buy you a cup of coffee or something. Have you eaten lunch? I'm buying."

Names are important to humans, Aeo interjected. *Introduce yourself.*

"My name is Val. What's yours?"

The woman continued to stare at him still in a defensive stance. Finally, she relaxed just a bit. "Willow," she replied. "I am kinda hungry, but I pick the place."

2

"WHY DID YOU PICK THE Student Union?" Val asked as he held the door open as Aeo had instructed for the woman who'd probably just ruined the MIT's football season. "There are much nicer places just a couple blocks away."

"Yeah, I know," Willow replied, "but I like pretending that I'm enrolled here. Just one of my flights of fancy. Besides, you give me any trouble, I'll just scream and get you kicked out of school."

"You'd do that?" Val asked.

"No, not really," Willow admitted. "I'd just kick your ass as I did to those boys back there. That's a lot more fun."

The two of them went through the cafeteria line with Willow piling her tray with food while Val just bought a large cup of iced tea.

"You really going to eat all that?" he asked, as he paid the lady behind the register.

"What? This? Did I break your weekly budget or something?"

"No. It's just that you don't look like you could eat that much food at one sitting."

"I said I was hungry. Besides, if I can't eat it all, I'll just get a doggie bag for later."

Val stared at her with a confused look on his face.

Doggie bag: a bag used by a restaurant customer or party guest to take home leftover food, supposedly for their dog, Aeo interjected.

"Oh, I see," Val replied. "What kind of dog do you have?"

"I don't, silly. It's just what people say when they plan to take food home. You know, you're kind of strange."

See, that's what I've been telling you, Aeo agreed. *We still have plenty of socializing skills on which to work.*

"Tell me a little about yourself," Val said, as much to change the subject as anything.

"Not much to tell," Willow said between mouthfuls of a corn beef sandwich. "Born a few blocks from these hallowed halls, but in the less desirable neighborhood. The only member of my family to ever finish high school. My mom kicked her husband out when I was three, so she couldn't afford to send me to college. So I started dropping in on classes that sounded interesting."

"And nobody objected?" Val asked.

"Not until those two idiots started pestering me."

"Where did you learn to fight like that?"

"Around," Willow replied. "As I said, my neighborhood isn't the nicest one in town. I learned pretty early that if I didn't want to spend my whole life on my back, I'd need to learn how to take care of myself. Last few years, I've been perfecting my craft through MMA."

"MMA?"

"Mixed Martial Arts?" Willow replied. "You must be one of those genius level eggheads that knows everything in the world, but not anything that's really useful, right?"

Val decided to ignore the question, concentrating on his tea instead.

They sat in silence for a few moments while Willow finished off the sandwich and then dug into her fries. She flipped the book that lay next to her tray open and pulled out a flyer that she'd been using as a bookmark. She slid it towards him. "I have a fight coming up this weekend. Feel free to check it out. I almost never have anyone there to cheer me on."

Val glanced down at the flyer, then back to Willow. "Sure, I guess. It's a...a date." *See, I've getting the hang of this culture.*

"No, it's not," Willow corrected him. "It's not a date. If you show, you show. No skin off of me either way."

As I said, you still need a lot of work, grasshopper.

Grasshopper? Why the hell are you referring to me as one of Earth's lowly insects? Val asked but Aeo only repeated. *Much work indeed.*

"Okay, not a date," Val said, picking up the flyer, folding it and placing it in his pocket, "but I'll be there. If you win the fight, we'll discuss the little business opportunity I mentioned."

"Not if, but when," Willow corrected him. "My fight is one of the last ones, so look me up at the end. We'll talk again," she said as she finished off the fries, then picked up the second sandwich. She looked at it as though trying to decide whether to start eating it or not, then wrapped it in a napkin instead, then picked up the book and stood up to leave.

"It'll make a good afternoon snack after my last class," she said.

"You're still planning to attend another class even after what happened with those thugs?"

"Sure thing. It takes a lot more than that to change my mind. See you around." And with that, she turned on her heels and strolled away.

I think we may have found the answer to our little dilemma, Aeo said.

Val nodded. *What did you find out about her?*

Very little, Aeo replied. *There's almost no information about her on the internet. She appears to be a classic case of a nobody...except with the Mixed Martial Arts where she has a reputation for being a dirty fighter with a nasty temper.*

Perfect.

Mixed Martial Arts

On the following Saturday evening, Val found his way to the Boston's Sports Arena with some assistance. Aeo provided directions through the narrow streets strewn with debris and more than their share of homeless people already settling in for the evening. It turned out that the Arena was an old warehouse that probably should have been torn down years ago, but someone had seen its potential as a location for the growing sport of Mixed Martial Arts. Val paid for a ticket and walked into the expansive building that was rapidly filling with avid fans of the sport.

As Val entered the main room, he saw in the center a large octagonal structure with mesh-like fencing around its perimeter running up about seven feet. The bleachers around it were already more than half full. *That's the cage where the fighting takes place*, Aeo said.

How do you know?

Why, the internet, of course.

Any suggestions on where I should sit? Val asked.

Not really, just somewhere you can see the action. According to the schedule, Willow will be the last fight of the evening.

Val found a spot about halfway up that would put him above the people walking around on the floor and more or less level with the cage. As he waited, he studied the crowd that seemed to be about an equal mix of men and women, most of them dressed in jeans and work shirts with several of them displaying images of their favorite fighters or other images related to the sport, but there was also another much smaller group. These were men dressed in suits, some wearing ties while others had open collars. Almost all of these men had one or more women with them dressed in slinky gowns that looked entirely out of place to Val.

Who the hell are those people? He asked nodding his head in their direction.

Not sure, Aeo answered. *I don't remember seeing anything about them. Give me a minute. Let me see what I can find.*

While Val waited, the first fight was announced by a large, overweight man dressed in a rumpled suit. He was sweating profusely. As he introduced the two fighters, two young girls with closely cropped hair and dressed in tight-fitting shorts and halter tops stepped into the octagon, staring hard at each other.

This is going to be more than just a staring match, isn't it? Val asked. *If not, I'm going home now.*

No, no. That's just their way to try to intimidate each other. Just wait, you'll see.

And see he did. Within a couple of minutes, the two women were clinging to each other as they rolled around on the floor trying to land a blow that would give them the advantage, while their opponent tried to protect herself from such a blow landing. The only other person in the ring was a muscular black man wearing a skin-tight t-shirt that showed off his well-endowed body. Around him, the other spectators hooted and cheered for the fighter they wanted to win.

Are they fighting or making love? Val asked.

Hard to tell, isn't it? But this is just one form that MMA takes. From what I can gather, the fighters who are not as well-trained tend to get into these clutches while the more experienced ones just try to knock their opponent out as fast as possible.

Really? Well, can we move on to one of those fights? Val asked. *I'd really like to go home and study my music appreciation.*

You would?

Hell no, but this is almost as boring as that drivel.

Patience...you must learn a little patience. It'll be over soon.

But unfortunately, Aeo was wrong. The first fight went the full three rounds with the fighters rolling around on the floor during each round. By the end, the crowd was booing both fighters. Finally, a bell sounded ending the fight. The referee spent a minute or two conferring with several other men along the side, then raised the arm of one of the women who'd spent the most time on top. A few fans cheered, but they were drowned out by the boos.

"Let's see a real fight!" Someone in the bleacher above Val shouted which brought on a cheer from the rest of the crowd.

As the second pair of fighters approached the cage, Aeo spoke up. *I found out who those well-dressed people are. They're either the organizers of the fight, or they are the fight owners and managers.*

Val nodded. *So, they're the ones making money out of this fiasco, right?*

Exactly.

Humans and their greed for money. How very trite, Val said, but even as he thought it, he realized it wasn't all that different on Allacria. The only real difference is that Allacrians far preferred power and new territories over something as simple as money, but in both cases, greed was the predominant driving force. In fact, as far as he could tell, it drove most of the galaxy.

He continued to watch with varying degrees of interest as the fights continued. True to Aeo's comment, with each fight, the quality improved. By the time the last fight had been announced, Val found he was actually enjoying the competition. He was especially looking forward to seeing his fighter climb into the ring.

She's not our fighter yet, Aeo pointed out.

Well, no, not technically, Val admitted, *but when she wins this fight, she will be.*

If she wins, Aeo corrected him.

Would you care to put a little wager on that? Besides watching the fights, Val had also been studying the crowd and realized that part of the fun from the spectators' perspective was betting with each other who would win. He decided it might add another dimension of pleasure to this last fight, besides which he did not doubt Willow's abilities. After all, she'd finished off those two thugs in less than a minute.

Well, actually I believe she'll win as well, Aeo admitted, *but if you'd enjoy the fight more by placing a small bet, I'm more than willing to play along. What should be the wager?*

Val thought a moment before replying. *If Willow wins, you agree to leave me alone for the rest of the month. Put yourself in suspension.*

And if she loses?

You name it.

You audit an art class for the rest of the semester, Aeo replied immediately.

What? You've got to be kidding.

Not at all. It would be quite helpful if you began to appreciate some of the finer points of this human culture.

But I'm already taking that damn music course, Val argued. *I'm really not interested in taking another worthless course like that.*

And I'm not interested in being in suspension for the rest of the month. That's what makes betting interesting. You have the chance to get something you want, but at the same time, you run the risk of losing something or having to do something you don't want.

Val thought about it for a moment. There was almost no chance that Willow would lose the match, so there was really very little risk on his part. *Okay, we have a bet.* Suddenly, this next fight had taken on a whole new level of interest and anticipation.

As the match was announced, the two fighters entered from opposite ends of the arena. Willow was once again dressed completely in black—black tight-fitting shorts that showed off her muscular legs, black halter top with matching black gloves that gave some protection to the hands while keeping the fingers free for grasping the opponent.

From the other end came the second fighter who was dressed in similar garb, but with a red and gold theme. She appeared to be several inches taller than Willow but equally well muscled. As she entered the room, a contingency of fans at the end broke into raucous cheers, chanting "Uma kicks ass...Uma kicks ass...and she'll kick yours tonight."

Below him, Val noticed several of the well-dressed men and women standing to cheer on their fighter as well. Clearly, this Uma woman was the favorite in tonight's fight. She certainly looked like she could hold her own against anyone else he'd seen fight tonight. She also radiated confidence, and a don't-fuck-with-me attitude. This fight could be closer than he'd first thought. He began to wonder what kind of art class Aeo would insist he take, then stopped himself. Willow would come through...right?

"This is the main event of the evening," the fat man in the rumpled suit announced from the center of the stage. "It's scheduled to go five rounds of five minutes each or until one of the fighters can no longer continue. Take it away, Jeremy."

The same black man that had been the referee of the earlier fights stepped forward to give the two women a few last minute instructions before sending them to opposite ends of the cage. A second later the bell rang, and the fight was underway.

The two fighters circled the cage the first thirty seconds sizing each other up as the crowd cheered them on. Uma made the first move with a flurry of blows to Willow's body before skipping back out of Willow's shorter reach. Willow blocked most of the blows with her arms and elbows and appeared no worse for it. Uma repeated the move twice more. The last time several of the blows made their way through Willow's defenses, landing squarely and taking their toil.

Go Uma! Aeo shouted, and Val winced at how loud it sounded in his head. If Uma kept this up, she'd wear Willow down. *It appears my fighter is going for a long game strategy. She realizes the fight is scheduled for five rounds instead of three, so she's going to wear her opponent down. Wise move,* Aeo remarked.

Her opponent is the fighter we intend to hire, Val pointed out though he had to agree that Uma's strategy seemed to be working. Willow was starting to show signs of fatigue from the assault of body blows. Was that a look of apprehension growing on her face?

Once again, Uma attacked the body, this time with a combination of blows and kicks, several of which landed even as Willow danced away. It began to look like Val would need to make room in his schedule for another boring class, but wait, what was that look on Willow's face now? Something had suddenly shifted subtly in her continence. For just a second, a slight smile had formed on her lips but then disappeared so fast Val wasn't even sure if he'd seen it or not.

Once again Uma attacked and once again Willow backed away but just as Uma finished her flurry of shots, Willow spun around, lifting her leg high in the air and catching her opponent in the head with the heel of her foot. Uma dropped to the matt without making a sound except a dull thud of her body landing hard. She lay on the canvas barely moving while Willow danced around her. The referee rushed in to check the downed fighter. After a moment, he raised his arms up and motioned that the fight was over. The crowd gasped in unison then broke out into a mixture of surprised boos and jeers. Willow raised her arms in a victorious salute as Uma slowly began to move around and then tried to stand up. Willow glided over before the referee could intervene and stomped on the other woman's head. She hit the deck again, even harder this time and lay still.

The referee jumped to pull Willow away as the crowd erupted in angry protest. The referee glanced over to the judge's table before waving his arms for attention. Over the sound of the loud crowd, he shouted, "The fighter has been disqualified for an illegal blow to the head. The winner by default is Uma Winslow."

The crowd cheered their pleasure and agreement. Willow stared, first at the referee, then at the judges, before shrugging and walking away.

What just happened? Val asked, stunned by the sudden outcome. Willow had been amazing, biding her time just waiting for the opening, then ending the fight with certainty, but what was that the referee had said about her being disqualified? That didn't make sense.

What happened? You just lost the bet, Aeo replied. *I'll get you a list of music classes from which you can choose. Now, find our girl and offer her a job.*

Job Offer

1

Val sent a note back to Willow that he'd wait for her out front to take her to dinner. Twenty minutes later, Willow exited the warehouse. She wore a short black skirt that once again highlighted her shapely legs and a matching black blouse. The belt of a fanny pack emphasized her slim waist. *I wonder if she even owns anything that's not black,* Val thought, but he had to admit, she did look good in black. He waved at her to draw her attention then sauntered towards her.

"That was an amazing fight," he said as he approached her. "Hardly seemed right that the referee disqualified you for just finishing it off."

Willow shrugged. "I'm not surprised. I lost my cool for just a minute. Uma and I go way back. We have history, most of it not good. It cost me some prize money that I could ill afford to lose, but it was worth it to see her hit the matt a second time. Now, your note said something about dinner?"

"Yeah," Val replied. "I've made reservations for two at Cuchi Cuchi restaurant, and I have a cab waiting for us. Right this way." Val waved one arm towards the waiting Yellow Cab."

"Cuchi's, huh? You're not making a move on me, are you?" Willow asked with a suspicious look mixed with a little smile on her face.

"Not at all," Val replied. "Purely business."

"So, we're finally going to talk about the opportunity you keep hinting about?"

"Promise, right after we order."

The two of them sat silently in the back of the cab on the short ride to the restaurant.

You need to work on your small talk, Aeo said.

What the hell is 'small talk?' I didn't think talking had any particular size, Val retorted.

Small talk is a colloquial term for casual conversation used to fill a period of silence. It's what you should be doing right now.

Why that's the dumbest thing I've heard in a long time. You mean, talking just to hear myself talk? Why would I want to waste my time in that way?

Because it's the polite thing to do, Aeo replied. *Besides, often you can find out more about the other person in such casual conversations.*

Wouldn't it just be simpler just to come right out and ask a direct question?

There was a long pause before Aeo replied, *I think you're missing the point. Humans are not always that forthcoming. They're often guarded about certain part of their lives.*

"You seem deep in thought," Willow said, catching Val by surprise.

"Oh, sorry," he replied. "I'm not much for making small talk."

"Good, me either. It's actually rather pleasant to just sit here and not have to think up something to say."

"I think we're going to get along just fine," Val replied. *Shistuon on small talk!* He directed to Aeo.

2

VAL AND WILLOW ARRIVED at the restaurant to find a table in a private dining room already set up for them. Beside the table was a bottle of Dom Perignon champagne with a note attached to the bottle. Val opened it to find a list of art classes along with a message:

Pick your course, and I'll add you to the class roster. Enjoy.

"What's that?" Willow asked, pointing to the note.

"Just a little joke from a colleague of mine," Val replied as he held Willow's chair out as Aeo had carefully schooled him previously.

They waited while the wine steward opened the champagne and poured each of them a glass while they perused the menus.

After the steward had left, Willow leaned over towards Val. "Where are the prices?" she whispered.

Val flipped through his menu before replying, "Hmm, I don't know. They seemed to have left them off my copy as well."

5-star restaurants don't bother their elite patrons with such trivial matters as pricing, Aeo offered. *Enjoy the meal. Our account will cover it.*

What account is that?

I opened a bank account a few days ago. Remember, the black card I gave you? Just hand that to the waiter when you're done. He'll take care of the rest. You did remember to bring the package I gave you too, right?

Of course, Val replied, tapping his coat pocket. *I'm not an idiot.*

He waited for some reply, but when he received nothing but silence, he turned his attention back to Willow who continued to study the menu.

She leaned over to him again. "Are you sure you can afford this place? I mean, after all, you're just a grad student, and all the grad students I've ever met had a pretty limited budget."

"And how many have you met?"

"Well, not that many I guess," Willow admitted. "Okay, three...counting you."

"Your other two friends might have been without funds, but I can assure you that is not the case with me."

Willow studied him for several seconds. "What kind of business opportunity are you offering me?"

Val chuckled at her obvious discomfort. "Enjoy your meal. We'll talk business afterward."

It was clear to Val that Willow was someone who knew how to take advantage of the opportunities offered to her. When it was time to order, she asked for the surf and turf that included lobster and a filet mignon. During the meal, the two of them finished off the bottle of champagne. When the bottle was turned over into the bucket, she frowned. "That's really good stuff. Do you think we could order another bottle?"

Val nodded and called the waiter who stood in the corner of the room over.

Finally, after they finished their respective desserts, Val ordered them cognac and coffee. When it arrived, he dismissed the waiter. After a few quiet moments, he reached into his jacket pocket and pulled out a thick stack of bills, placed it on the table and slid it in Willow's direction.

Willow put down her glass of cognac and stared at the stack. "What's that?" She finally asked.

"Consider it your retainer for service to be rendered in the future," Val replied.

Willow picked up the stack of bills to examine it more closely. "There must be over a thousand dollars here."

"Five thousand," Val corrected her.

"O...kay..." Willow replied as she flipped through the crisp bills. "Who do I have the kill?"

Val chuckled, "Don't be silly. No one," and he heard Aeo add, *least not yet*. "I'm in the midst of a very important project, one in which from time to time I might need a little assistance...let's say a little persuasion power. I believe you could prove quite valuable in that regard."

"You mean like persuading someone to see your point of view using my fists?"

"Or your feet or some combination, yes," Val replied. "For example, I have a graduate advisor that thinks he's found some irregularities in my records. It's not a big deal, but he's threatening to get me tossed out of school. That would be an unfortunate setback I'd just as soon avoid."

Willow placed the stack of money back down on the table but didn't slide it back towards him. She tapped one finger lightly on it instead as she considered the offer.

"What are you really up to?" she finally asked.

"Pardon?" The question caught Val by surprise. "What do you mean?"

"I mean, it seems unlikely that you're prepared to spend five grand just for me to persuade a college professor to overlook some record irregularities, so what are your really planning?"

Val studied her for several seconds before replying. "Oh, that. Well, I'm out to take over the world, of course."

3

The two of them stared at each other while Willow continued the tap, tap, tap on the stack of money. Finally, she laughed. "Well, in that case, I'm in!" she said, the stack of bills disappearing so quickly Val wasn't sure where it had gone. "So, now what?"

Val smiled and picked up his cognac. He sniffed it for a moment before taking a sip. "There's another grad student, a young woman, Melissa Porter. We have the same advisor. The two of them meet at his office late at night twice a week. I happen to know this Melissa woman has a boyfriend who would not be thrilled to find out about these late night visits."

"So you're going to blackmail your advisor?" Willow asked.

"No, at least not yet. I need to get on Professor Dinwiddle's good side. Make him owe me in some way. That way, maybe I can get him to reconsider his plan to report me."

"Dinwiddle? That's your advisor?"

Val nodded.

"Stupid name," Willow remarked. "So what do you want me to do?"

"I'm setting up a little late night meeting. I'm going to invite Eddie Valcro, that's Melissa's boyfriend, to drop by to meet his competition. I figure there's a good chance Eddie will not appreciate what's going on behind his back. When Eddie goes to take the professor apart, I'll be there to step in and protect my dear advisor. I just want you to be there in case something goes wrong."

Willow tapped the money in her lap. "That's it?" Val nodded. "No problem then. Just tell me when and where. I'll be there."

Val wrote down the information on a slip of paper and handed it to her. She took the paper and held out her hand. Val stared at it. "What's that for?" he finally asked.

"To shake on our deal," Willow replied. "You're weird; you know that? What planet are you from anyway?"

Before Val could say anything, Aeo shouted, *Don't answer that question!*

Val closed his mouth and smiled. Standing up, he waved a hand for the waiter to return. "I'll pay the bill and have someone call you a cab. It's been a pleasure, Ms. Crowe. I'll see you in a few days."

"What? That's it? You're not going to share the cab with me?"

"No. I like to walk off a heavy meal like this. Now, if you'll excuse me, I need to find the restroom."

Willow sat at the table until the waiter and Val had left the room, then pulled a cell phone from her fanny pack. She tapped in a number and waited until someone answered on the other end. "I'm in," she said, then disconnected the call without waiting for a reply.

Part Two

Back on Land

1

After the pod of dolphins had driven the sharks away from Todd, several of them circled, nuzzling him as though examining him for possible injuries, but the only wound he'd acquired throughout the accident had been a small laceration to the head which had already started to scab over and heal. But it didn't take them long to determine that the dolphin they'd just rescued was not only exhausted but was more than a little bit strange, especially in the scent it gave off—a combination of dolphin, bird, and human. Perhaps it was this combination of these unusual scents along with the exhaustion that helped Todd communicate the need to return to land as soon as possible, but before he knew it, they were headed in a northwesterly direction.

While a pod of healthy dolphins could typically cover the distance back to shore in a little over two days, they could not travel at their normal speed for extended lengths of time without leaving Todd far behind. So, they moved more slowly, taking frequent breaks. Often, when they resumed their journey, several of the dolphins would take turns swimming below him, thus partially supporting his weight and making it easier for him to swim.

Never thought I'd have to resort to piggy-back rides on a dolphin to survive, Todd thought, but he was thankful that such an altruistic species lived in the ocean. He'd read stories of how dolphins helped sailors from drowning, but he'd always chalked them up as sentimental fables. Now he knew better.

For four days, the pod remained with him, taking occasional breaks to rest, even partially supporting him when they swam as he acclimated to his new form and surroundings. During this time, he never noticed any of the dolphins actually sleep. It wasn't until towards the end of the four days that he figured out how they managed this. By that time, he'd begun to acquire more of a sense of "dolphin-hood" for himself which included being able to sense the dolphins around him. He noticed a difference among some of them, finally determining that some of the dolphins were only half awake while the other half of their brain rested. They appeared to take turns at this with a few of the dolphins always being fully awake while the others partially slept. Unfortunately, he was only partially successful at learning this trick. His being able to do this, even partially, alerted him that he was slowly taking on more of the qualities of the dolphin form. He would need to transform back to human form as soon as possible unless he wanted to spend the rest of his life as a dolphin. It was a thought that caused him to pause and ponder it a bit as he observed the selflessness, care, and compassion of the pod. He could think of worst fates, but finally decided he'd miss too many of the luxuries of human life. Small things like eating as many Cheerios as he wanted, walks out in nature and watching sunrises and sunsets.

So, at the end of the fourth day, as they finally reached the coast, he said goodbye to the pod of dolphins. Even so, he knew he'd learned much about this noble species as well as how truly useful such a form was likely to prove down the road. After the pod had swum back out to sea, Todd traveled along the coast looking for a secluded spot where he could morph back to human form without being detected, while at the same time not being too far from civilization. The former was more challenging than the latter since so much of the coast along this stretch was well developed with row after row of beachfront cottages. He finally found a stretch of beach without any houses. He was becoming increasingly concerned that he'd not be able to change back to his original form, so he decided he'd have to chance being detected. He beached himself on the sand and began the morphing process back to human. Indeed, the process was slow at first, as his makeup had grown comfortable with the dolphin form and he was still tired from the last few days' ordeal. But slowly his body remembered the composition of a human being and the transition occurred with only mild discomfort.

The next order of business was to acquire some clothes before he was arrested for indecent exposure, but that wasn't too difficult. Someone who was staying in one of the older beachfront cottages had left several articles of clothing hanging on the line to dry. Todd waited behind a dune until the sun had set sufficiently that he could avoid detection, then quickly clamored forward, grabbed several pieces that looked like they'd come close to fitting, along with a couple of beach towels and then scurried back to the dunes.

The next order of business was to get some rest. While his friends the dolphins had done an excellent job feeding him, he was still far from a hundred percent. A good night sleep would help clear his mind as well as rejuvenate his body. Come morning, he would figure out where he'd come to shore, then dig up some grub and...and then what? He wasn't sure. He was too tired to give it much thought tonight. Tomorrow would be soon enough to sort out such a question.

2

TODD AWOKE THE NEXT morning stiff and cold and with sand having seeped into every crack and crevice of his body—a body that already smelled like a mixture of rotten fish and seaweed left wilting in the sun too long. He needed a good bath, but even more urgent was something to eat. The trials and tribulations of the past several days had taken their toll. He realized that the main reason the stolen clothes hung on him was that he'd lost a good ten pounds since the helicopter crash. *Could have lost a lot more than that*, he mused recalling the close call with the sharks.

As he stood up and attempted to stretch out the kinks in his limbs, he pondered his situation. All he owned were the stolen clothes on his back. He had no food and worse, no money to buy any. Even when he'd run away to Asheville, he'd managed to borrow, okay steal, a little money before heading out. Not only was he homeless once again, but this time he was also penniless. Starting life over with a clean set suddenly didn't look so appealing.

He walked to the top of the dune and looked around until he located the closest road. All roads eventually led to some town or village. The question was, in which direction was the closest one where he could start this grand life of his over again? He would flip a coin to decide which direction to walk except that he didn't have one to flip. Instead, he walked down to the road. Standing in the middle of it, he spun around several times until he became dizzy, then stopped to see which direction he was heading—more or less north. Then that's the direction he'd head.

By the position of the sun just rising out of the ocean, he estimated it was probably close to seven or seven-thirty, and so far there was still only a few cars on the road. He thought about trying to hitch a ride but then thought better of it. He smelled too bad and besides, he'd run the risk of someone asking too many questions—questions that he was ill-equipped to answer. Luckily, he only walked a mile or two when the number of cottages began to increase, which hopefully meant he wasn't too far from some town. Walking a little further, he came upon a combination gas station and convenience market that was already open, though with few customers. He headed to the bathroom where he relieved himself and then did what he could to clean up using the hand soap and paper towels he found there. That would have to do for now. Walking back out, he grabbed the first food he saw, a box of doughnuts, then scurried back to the bathroom where he devoured them, hiding the evidence in the trash can. That would have to hold him for a bit until he could come up with a better plan. He left the store, ignoring the old lady's suspicious stare behind the counter.

Perhaps it was Providence looking after him, or just the law of averages beginning to balance all his bad luck with a little bit of good fortune, but he calculated it was less than two miles further down the road when he came upon the Biddle Circus and Vaudeville Acts. It looked as though the circus was also new to the area as the main tent was still laying flat on the ground waiting to be erected. But Todd saw not a huge piece of worn canvas in need of constructing. Instead, he saw his next full meal and who knew, maybe more.

He strolled towards the clump of men gathered near the tent, several of them holding sledge hammers while others had thick strands of rope looped over their shoulders. "Good morning, gents. It looks like you've got your work cut out for you this fine morning. Could you use a hand?"

A couple of the large men dressed in blue jeans and work shirts glanced at another smaller man wearing a clean white shirt and khaki pants, obviously the boss of the group. "Yeah, sure. A couple of our crew are out sick this morning. Can't pay you much, but as soon as the kitchen RV arrives, I'll see you get a good breakfast." He held out his hand. "I'm Odie Stickney, though most people just call me Buzz."

Todd shook hands and nodded. "Seems fair to me," Todd said as he picked up one of the hammers lying on the ground. "Let's get to it."

Allan's "Anniversary"

1

Allan sat staring into his old fashion, the ice half melted with the partially chewed orange slice laying in the bottom of the glass. It was two years to the day since he and Pat had split, and he'd found himself driving around aimlessly at night, finally lighting at the Suds and Duds on the outskirts of Black Mountain, over an hour from his home. It had seemed like a haven to tie one on without any of his clients interrupting him with senseless veterinary questions.

He had returned each year on this date, though he didn't know exactly why. He felt reasonably normal most of the other 364 days of the year, except for the occasional interruption, as had happened a couple of days ago when he'd uncovered TJ's handwritten message in the bottom of his sock drawer. He'd almost started drinking then but decided at the last minute to wait a couple of days until he could 'celebrate' in his accustomed manner.

He took a couple of swallows of his drink before waving it at Marjorie, the bartender, and owner of the combination bar and laundromat.

"Another?" Marjorie asked from the other end of the bar. Allan nodded. "Coming right up. You want me to call down to the Red Rocker Inn to see if they have a room?"

Allan shook his head. "Already booked one," he replied. The last thing he needed to do was to try to drive home along the winding mountain roads between Black Mountain and Waynesboro. After a minute, Marjorie walked his third drink over to him. "How many years does this make?" she asked as she set the drink down in front of him and picked up his empty one.

"This is my third year here," Allan replied.

"So, two years since the split, right?" Marjorie asked.

Allan nodded.

"You think maybe it's time you got on with your life?" Marjorie said as she picked up a towel and pretended to clean the bar next to where Allan sat.

"Yeah, maybe," Allan replied, then looked at the attractive blonde. "You want to be my girlfriend?" He smiled to let her know he was only joking.

"Sure, just let me check with Jake to make sure he doesn't mind."

After the bartender left to wait on another customer, her question continued to bounce around in Allan's thoughts. She's probably right. What was the point of revisiting the past like this, especially such a downer part? Those weeks after Pat had found the note from TJ alerting them to his running away had been some of the most traumatic of Allan's life. What followed had been weeks of searching for him in Asheville assisted by one of Pat's P. I. colleagues, Shack Lawson, but to no avail. As the days passed into weeks, Allan began to feel something wasn't quite right. Finally, he decided to do a little detective work of his own. On one of his Wednesday afternoons off, he drove to Asheville to pay Lawson an unannounced visit. He planned to catch the P. I. by surprise, hoping he'd reveal something...anything that would give Allan a new lead as to TJ's whereabouts. Unfortunately, Shack was less than helpful, claiming he couldn't reveal anything without his client's permission.

"But I am your client," Allan insisted.

"No, Pat hired me, not you," Shack replied, leaning back in his chair behind his desk.

"But she hired you to find my son," Allan insisted.

"Yes, that's correct. So, talk to her. I can't help you."

Allan still remembered how angry he'd become, jumping out of his chair to charge the P. I. Shack hadn't even flinched but continued to stare at him with a benevolent smile on his face. "What are you doing?" he finally asked. "Go home, Dr. Pritchard. Fix yourself a drink and chill out."

Leaning across the desk that separated the two men, Allan stared back at Shack, the anger slowly seeping out of him. "I need to find TJ," he finally said in a voice little more than a whisper.

Shack straightened up in his chair. "I understand. I really do. Like I said before, go home and talk to Pat."

There'd been something in the way Shack had said that last sentence that haunted Allan all the way on the drive home.

2

PAT WASN'T DUE BACK from a business trip for a couple of days which gave Shack's last words plenty of time to seep into his mind while awake and even in his sleep. By the time the evening of her return had arrived, Allan had resolved to take the P. I.'s advice with just a little twist. Everything started out as a regular return with Allan doing his best to act excited to see her. For his plan to work, it required that she be taken by surprise. So, even though he felt like a fraud/heel, he performed his best acting role since starring in his high school play more years ago than he cared to remember.

After dinner, they took their glasses of wine into the den as was their custom, but Allan decided to forego turning on the television or music. The time had arrived to spring the trap. He took a moment to say a silent prayer then launched into it.

"Guess who I ran into the other day?" he started, then promptly kicked himself. That wasn't how he wanted to start. He tried again. "It wasn't an accidental meeting. I'd planned it."

"What are you talking about?" Pat asked, sitting up a little straighter and studying Allan's face.

Shit, she's already suspicious. It's hard to put anything over on someone whose job is to snoop out other people's lies and deceptions. Okay, it's time for a full out assault. "I'm talking about what I learned from talking to the P. I. In Asheville."

"You mean Shack?" Pat asked, then added, "How's the old pervert doing these days?"

"No doubt, feeling much better," Allan countered. "You know what they say about confession being good for the soul."

"Confession?" Pat asked, her voice cracking just a bit. "What on earth are you talking about?"

Allan stood up and started pacing around the room to burn off some of the angry energy that was building inside him. "He told me everything about what you did. Spilled his guts, he did. Of course, it took me bribing him to get him to start. But you know the power of money when it comes to making greedy people do what you want." Allan paused for effect before adding. "What do you have to say for yourself?"

Now shut up and let her talk, Allan thought. The silence dragged on. He continued to stand in the middle of the floor staring at her accusingly like he'd seen television attorneys do so many times just before the real criminal broke down and confessed. The silence ticked by, but Pat continued to sit there with her wine glass suspended halfway to her lips, her eyes focused on his. Who would break the staring match first?

Maybe I should say something? Drive my point across just a little more. No! Shut up. It's her turn. The next person to speak loses. Loses? Is that what our relationship has become, a game of win or lose? Allan knew the answer to that question was an unequivocal yes.

"I did it for us," Pat finally said just before taking a sip of her wine, then added. "And I'd do it again."

Was that a confession? Allan wondered. Well, yes, sorta, but a confession to what? Time to dig a little deeper.

"You would, would you?"

"Yes." It was Pat's turn to stand up and start pacing. "I knew if we were to have any future together, it had to be one without TJ in the picture. You've become blind when it comes to TJ."

"So, you took it on yourself to see to it that TJ would be out of my life, just like that?" Allan could feel the anger growing and starting to come out in his words. Stay calm, he thought. Anger never solves anything.

"Yes I did," Pat replied, her voice rising in pitch and volume. Clearly, her own anger was beginning to take over as well. "Don't you see, Allan? I did it because I love you, and I want us to have a future together, but that can't happen with TJ in the picture."

Allan turned away to control his temper. What had she done to get TJ out of the picture? After all, she had military training and was a P. I. with all sorts of shady connections. Was TJ lying in some shallow grave somewhere...somewhere on his property? No, she wouldn't do such thing, would she? Maybe not, but she might have someone else take care of the matter. No, this is crazy. This is Pat, the woman I love. But did he love her anymore after what she'd just confessed? He slowly turned around to face her again.

"Let me make one thing perfectly clear. Whatever you think of TJ, who he is, what he is, I love him as a son. That's the way it is, and if you can't deal with that, then we have no future together. Do you understand?"

The two of them stood face to face staring at each other for close to a minute. Finally, Pat nodded, finished off her glass of wine and placed it on the coffee table. "Perfectly," she said. "I'll be out of your house and your life by morning." And with that she strolled out of the room, leaving Allan alone.

As always, Pat had been true to her word. She had packed up her belongings and left sometime during the night. That had been over two years ago, and Allan had neither seen nor heard from her since. He also still didn't know exactly what she'd done to eliminate TJ from their lives. Allan had finally decided it didn't really matter. If he was still alive, TJ knew where to find Allan. He'd find his way home if and when it was time. And if TJ was dead...well, he tried not to think about that. Such thoughts only drove him to drink that much more.

Firefly

The big top rose into the morning sky faster than Todd had anticipated, but there was still plenty to do to make sure it was securely fastened to the sandy soil of the coast. He found himself working next to another man a few years older and several inches shorter, though he suspected they probably weighed close to the same weight. To put it simply, the man was built like a brick shit house, and his muscles were much appreciated by the rest of the crew, who called on him frequently when a little extra muscle was needed. As they worked, additional vehicles pulled into the open field, including some horse trailers. A large RV with a painting of dogs jumping through hoops and performing other tricks on it pulled in behind the trailers. A few moments later, the grub truck pulled in, which was the most popular vehicle of all, especially among the workers.

"Hey, Firefly, give us a hand unloading the horses, will you?"

"Sure thing, boss man," the man next to Todd yelled back, then glanced over at him. "You want to give me a hand?"

Todd nodded, handing the sledgehammer to another worker.

"You're not nervous around horses, are you?" Firefly asked as they walked towards the trailer.

Todd shook his head. "I'm comfortable around most animals," he replied. "My dad was a vet, so I have at least a passing knowledge of how to act around them." *Not to mention I can morph into a fair number of their forms,* Todd thought, smiling to himself.

"Good," Firefly replied. "These horses are easy to work with for the most part. A bit high strung at times, like most entertainers, but Dessi has done an excellent job training them. That's her over there." Firefly pointed to a slender young woman with a golden crest of curls encircling her face climbing out of one of the cabs.

Todd stared at her for several seconds. She wore tight-fitting jeans that accentuated her shapely legs and a loose-fitting blouse of fabric that was just barely see through. "Nice," Todd muttered.

"You can say that again," Firefly agreed. "Nice to look at and even nicer to be around, but I'd be careful. Rumor has it that Buzz and she have something going. You don't want to get on the boss's wrong side."

"Why's that? He seems okay."

"Yeah, for the most part, he is...except when he isn't. He's got a bit of a drinking problem. Now, don't get me wrong. I'm not a prude. When it comes to booze, I like to down my share. Most circus hands do. It helps to relieve the sore muscles and tension that naturally builds up over time. The trouble is, Buzz has more than his share of tension and worries. It's not easy keeping a circus going these days. Anyway, you're still staring."

Todd blushed and looked away, but found his eyes kept straying back to take in just a second or two more of the beauty named Dessi. Finally, she stepped around one of the trucks and out of sight, finally releasing Todd to join Firefly in unloading the horses. There were six of them, all gorgeous white Arabians, who'd obviously been receiving the very best of care.

"By the way, I'm Firefly," the man said, holding out his hand. Todd noticed a simple tattoo of two military dog tags on his forearm. Inscribed on one of the tags was "All Gave Some," and on the other, "Some Gave All."

"I'm..." Todd paused. Who the hell was he now...now that Sergeant Todd John Jacobs was dead? "Todd," he finally finished. He'd have to work out the details of his identity later. For now, he'd try to get by with just a first name. "You ex-military?" he asked as much to redirect the attention away from his stammering as anything.

"Sure am," Firefly replied as he closed the door of the trailer. "You hang around until supper tonight, and I'll introduce you to a couple of the other grunts who have found a home here. You know what they say. If you can't hack real life, run away to the circus. Well, some of us didn't much care for what we found after our stint in the military, so we ended up here."

Interesting, Todd thought. He'd thought the military was going to be his home after it was clear he could no longer live with Allan and Pat. So, maybe he was looking for another home, but running away to the circus? That sounded even more juvenile than growing up to be a soldier of fortune. As he thought about finding a new home, Dessi strolled around the trailer and smiled at him. Her emerald green eyes glittered in the morning sunlight, and her wide smile was breathtakingly gorgeous. Then again, maybe circus life wasn't such a bad idea after all.

"Eyes over here, soldier," Firefly said, chuckling softly.

"I'm not..." Todd started to deny any connection to the military but then thought better of it. "How did you know?" he asked instead.

"Oh, I don't know. The way you carry yourself, the fact that you recognized my tattoo for where it came from. That and I'm psychic."

"You are?" Todd asked, a shocked look on his face.

"Of course not." Firefly laughed. "Just pretty good at reading people. If I were psychic, I'd say that your heart has already been entrapped by Ms. Dessi's aura."

"Ahh, well..." Todd found himself stuttering again. He glanced over at Firefly, looking for some way to change the subject. "Hey, I don't recognize that green emblem on your cap. Is that military? It reminds me a bit of one of those medical symbols?"

"A caduceus? No. It's not medical or military." Firefly chuckled again. "It's a firefly. You know, from the *Firefly* television show and movie. It's obviously also where I got my nickname. I loved that show. It's a shame they took it off the air after just two number of seasons. You'll find most of the people around here go by their nicknames. I guess it's our futile attempt to put our past in the past."

"That makes sense," Todd replied. "Any chance you could forget my name?"

Firefly stared at him hard for several seconds before replying. "Yeah, I could probably do that," he finally replied. "Everyone deserves a second chance in my book. Of course, that means we'll have to come up with a nickname."

"What would you suggest?" Todd asked, relieved by his new friend's acceptance.

"Don't know...not yet, but something will come to me. Just give me some time. Are you staying for supper?"

"Yeah, I guess so...if that's okay with boss man," Todd replied.

"Okay, good. I'll let you know your new name by then," Firefly promised. "Now, let's go check on the lions. They're a scruffy bunch, but they won't be with us much longer, so I like to check in on them whenever we've moved to a new location." The two of them started walking towards another larger tractor trailer. As they approached, Todd heard the growl of several large cats.

"PETA's been driving Buzz crazy over the lions. I believe it's been a major contributor to his drinking. Says they're not well treated and such. It's not true. I've never seen wild animals treated so well, but despite it all, Buzz finally agreed to send them to an animal sanctuary at the end of this year's run. Soon there will just be the horses and trained dogs. Of course, they're more popular these days, anyway. Still, I'm going to miss the lions, especially Reginald. What a majestic beast he is, even for his age."

The two men reached the trailer in time to watch as several other workers were unloading four cages, each one with a lion inside. "So, who takes care of the animals?" Todd asked.

"Well, I guess we all do," Firefly replied, "But none of us are really trained. We could really use someone who knows something about their care and feeding. You interested?"

Todd shrugged. He'd had a little experience with horses, mostly little factoids he picked up from Allan and what he could learn from the internet. Dogs, on the other hand, he was much more intimate with since it had been the earliest form he'd learned to morph into. Large cats were another matter entirely. Other than one or two barn cats that stayed around Allan's country home, he knew very little about them. Still, they'd be heading to the animal sanctuary before too long. He could probably fake it in the meantime. After all, becoming the animal caretaker might give him for opportunity to be around the horses' owner. He could think of worse fates. "Maybe," he finally answered. "While I'm here, I'll help out any way I can."

"Good," Firefly replied. "That's the right attitude to have around here. Most everyone is a bit of a Jack-of-all-trade. The more you can do, the more valuable you are, and the less likely you'll be the next one laid off." Before Todd had a chance to ask about that last comment, Firefly went on. "Ahh, I figured we might run into Python here. Let me introduce you to one of the other Army grunts."

They walked up to a tall, slender man wearing cowboy boots and the customary jeans and a red and black plaid work shirt. As they came closer, Todd noticed the boots were made from what appeared to be genuine snakeskin. He pointed to the boots. "Is that the reason for his name?"

"Yeah," Firefly answered back, then in a softer voice continued. "But I wouldn't say anything about them. They're his last pair. He told me once when he was three sheets to the wind that he used to spend his drug dealing money buying them. He had quite a collection. That is until he learned how many thousands of snakes are killed each year for the boot industry. Python is as tough a soldier as you'll find, but he's also a real animal lover at heart. Reginald is also one of his favorites."

"Easy there, fellas. Our king of the jungle is old and cranky these days. Let's not drop him. He might crack in half," Python shouted to the other workers who appeared to ignore his plea.

"He's not all that fragile," Firefly said as he walked up to the other man. "If you don't believe it, just stick your arm through those bars and see what happens."

Python turned to him and smiled. "No thanks. I've grown used to both of my arms, thank you very much."

"I want you to meet our latest addition." Firefly pointed to Todd. "We're still working on a name so until we come up with something perfect for him, meet New Boy."

Python eyed Todd up and down, then finally took a step in his direction and shook hands.

"Plenty of work to go around. The pay sucks big time, but the food is plentiful and mostly edible. Welcome aboard." The two men shook hands before Python turned back to the lion cages. "I'm going to miss these guys, but hey, I hear the sanctuary is like going to heaven on earth."

"Yeah, more like the Paradise promised to terrorists," Firefly quipped. "What is it, they'll find something like seventy-two virgins awaiting them?"

"Yeah, something like that," Python replied. "Not for me. Who wants to spend all eternity teaching virgins how to make love? No, give me seventy-two experienced women. Hell, one or two dozen would be more than enough."

Suddenly, Todd felt like he was back in his old Army barracks. Who knew?. Maybe he would stay around beyond supper tonight.

As the three men walked along the side of the cages, the lions were pulled to a second tent where they'd remain on display until the matinee show the next day. Todd saw Dessi exercising one of her horses across the way. Seventy-two virgins? No, he wasn't interested in owning a harem. One nice lady with a beautiful head of hair and a smile to die for would make him a pretty happy camper right now. For a moment, the face of Mimi Rawlings flashed across the motion picture of his mind. It had been quite a while since he'd thought of the young girl he'd had such a crush on as a teenager. Why would her image suddenly reappear as he stared at Dessi? *Maybe it means I'm ready to put her in the past and get on with another aspect of this new life before me.*

A Circus Dinner

As Todd walked into the tent that had been raised to serve as the circus' dining hall, he felt tired and in need of a shower, but he also felt like he'd put in a good day's work. It had been a good first day of his new life. As he stood in the entranceway, the first thing he noticed was that all the workers, many of whom he'd worked beside throughout the day, were all seated to the far right of the tent, while another group that appeared to be made up entirely of performers, was seated to the far left.

That's odd, he thought. Was this a family divided that he was about to join? He was still wondering what it was all about when he noticed Firefly waving to him from across the room. He waved back and walked over to find his new friend had saved him a seat. He nodded to Python who was also seated at the table next to another man he didn't recognize but looked vaguely familiar. He sat down next to Firefly, wondering where he'd seen the odd looking fellow next to Python, then he dawned on him where—in the ocean just a few days ago. The man looked just like one of the Great Whites that had almost made Todd its dinner. So, he wasn't at all surprised when Firefly introduced him.

"This is Shark, another disillusioned grunt that found himself attracted to the vagabond life of the circus." Todd reached across the table to shake the offered hand, half expecting to feel the sandpaper quality he'd felt when one of the sharks had brushed up against him. Instead, Shark's hand felt like any other worker with a firm grip that accentuated the hand's calluses.

"Good to meet you," Todd said.

"What's your name?" Shark asked.

"We've been calling him New Boy," Firefly answered. "Figured we'd come up with an appropriate nickname during supper."

Todd smiled and nodded to the other men sitting at the table. He noticed the kitchen help putting out the last few containers of food and several of the performers beginning to move towards the line of food. "Maybe we should hold off on that until after we get our food."

"Nah, there's no hurry," Python replied. "Performers get the first crack at the food since they often have to get ready for a show. We get what's left over, but don't worry, they've never run out of food yet."

"So, nominations are now open for naming New Boy," Firefly said. "Who's got one?"

There was a moment of silence then Python spoke up. "I've watched him off and on throughout the day. He's a hard worker, so maybe something like Dynamo?"

"Okay. Our first nomination is Dynamo. Who's got another?"

Todd noticed he was surprisingly nervous about what was happening around him. He knew from his Army days that a bad nickname could follow you everywhere and could give new people either a good or bad impression. But he figured he could live with Dynamo. He started to suggest closing the nominations, but before he could do so, FireFly spoke up.

"I've been thinking about this all day and watching New Boy myself. He's been really taken by our Miss Dessi."

"Who hasn't?" one of the men at the other end of the table said, and everyone laughed.

"True, but I got a feeling he's been lovestruck more than the rest of us," Firefly continued. "So how about something like Lover Boy or Moonstruck?"

Several of the men chuckled as they tried out the name. Todd suppressed a groan. He'd hate to go around with either name.

"Okay, let's see. We have Dynamo, Lover Boy, and Moonstruck on the list so far. Are there any other nomi..." Firefly stopped as he noticed Dessi enter the tent, but instead of heading to the performers' area, walked straight towards their table.

She wore the same clothes from earlier in the day, and there was a light layer of dirt on her face. Even so, it didn't diminish the warm glow she radiated as she strolled towards them. She nodded. "Good evening, Gents. I understand you've had a new man join your ranks. Is that right?"

"Good evening, Miss Dessi," Firefly answered as spokesperson. "That's right." He pointed to Todd. "In fact, we were just in the process of naming him."

Dessi nodded and smiled. "I see. And can anyone place a nomination?"

Firefly glanced around the table and saw no objection, but instead, just a lot of dumbstruck looks on his fellow workers replied. "Why sure. I don't see why not."

Dessi turned her gaze to Todd, and he felt his breath catch just a bit. "I was told you'd be helping to take care of the animals. Make sure they're fed properly and that they're bedded down properly. Is that correct?"

Todd nodded. "Yes, ma'am. I'd be happy to oblige."

"Good. The animals deserve it, and we need someone who can be responsible for their care. Why not come around to the horse trailers after dinner so we can go over matters?"

Todd nodded again, but was afraid if he tried to say anything his voice would crack or he'd say something even more stupid than 'yes ma'am.'"

Dessi turned to leave, but then stopped. "How about Caretaker for his name? Good evening fellows."

Caretaker was the unanimous winner when the voting was done. No one at the table wanted word to get back to Miss Dessi Stockton that they'd voted against her name. Todd, aka Caretaker, was satisfied as well even though, in hindsight, he figured Moonstruck might have been more accurate.

Rendezvous

Val glanced at his cellphone. 7:55. He'd told Willow to meet him in front of the professor's office building at 8. He looked up and down the street but still no Willow. Was she going to take the money and run? Aeo had assured him that wouldn't happen, but now it was looking like his "colleague" had misjudged her. Well, no matter. He'd texted Eddie Valcro a few minutes ago and almost immediately received a return text asking who he was. Val hesitated for a moment before texting back his name and how he knew about Melissa and Professor Dinwiddle.

A minute or so later he received a return text:

Thanks. I'll handle it. I owe you one.

The wheels were moving with or without his backup.

"Boo!" Val jumped, swinging around, unsure whether to run or fight. A laughing Willow stepped out of the shadows.

"What the hell was that about?" Val shouted, holding his phone against his chest.

"Oh, nothing," Willow replied, stifling the laughter down to a chuckle. "Just feeling playful. Ready when you are."

"Okay," Val replied a little calmer. "Let me just jump start my heart, and we'll proceed with the plan." After another moment to catch his breath, he brought his accomplice up to speed and proceeded to outline the plan. "We'll go around back to where the fire escape is. Dinwiddle's office will probably be the only one that's lit at this time of night. Earlier in the day, I jimmied the back door open and suggested Eddie go in that way. He should be here any minute so let's get in our position."

As they walked to the rear of the building, Willow asked, "So, just to confirm, I'm not to do anything unless you call for backup. Right?"

"That's right," Val replied. "You're just here in case Eddie is crazier than I think, and I can't control him. I don't anticipate that happening, so you should have an easy go tonight."

Val didn't bother mentioning that this was as much a test to determine Willow's reliability as anything. Her showing up was a good sign that she was on the team. Aeo had assured him that she'd be a much-needed asset as the mission unfolded.

As they approached the rear of the old academic building, Val pointed to the lone light on the fourth floor. "That's his office. Let's go."

"You sure? What if that's someone else working late tonight and your prof is rolling around in the dark with the other grad student?"

Val turned to glare at her. "I double checked earlier today to be sure. Also, I don't think they're actually having an affair. I fabricated that part of the story. Remember?"

Willow shrugged. "Okay. Just checking. I want to be sure I'm doing my part."

The two of them started climbing the fire escape with Val leading the way. They were almost to the fourth floor when they heard an automobile pull into the alley below. Val turned and looked down. "That's probably our Eddie right on time."

Willow nodded. "Did you check to be sure the office window wasn't locked?"

Val groaned. He hadn't thought of that. He had remembered the window was open the last time he'd met with Dinwiddle, but the temperatures had dropped these last few days. What if the professor had closed and locked it? They'd be trapped on the fire escape without a way to stop Eddie if he went ballistic on Melissa, the professor, or both. "It'll be unlocked," Val replied with more confidence than he felt. *Please be unlocked*, he thought as they continued their climb.

As they reached the professor's office, Val breathed a sigh of relief to find the window cracked open about six inches. That would be enough for them to listen in on the conversations and also be able to open it further when it was time to play the hero.

Val turned to Willow and raised one finger to his lips and pointed to the open window. She nodded as she joined him on the landing. Val noticed her movements were fluid and graceful and most importantly, quiet. The two of them situated themselves on either side of the window where they could see in without drawing attention. Inside, Professor Dinwiddle sat behind his desk while Melissa stood on the other side. They were both looking over some papers on the desk and discussing them.

"Too bad they're not rolling around on the floor making love," Willow whispered, smiling broadly.

"Why's that?" Val whispered back.

"More likely to cause a brawl with boyfriend Eddie."

Hmm, good point, Val thought. What if Eddie figured out that nothing was going on here and then just turned around and walked off?

Don't worry, Aeo piped in. *I checked around and found out that Eddie has a standing date with some of his buddies at the local pub. He'll be intoxicated and even more irrational than usual.*

Val hoped Aeo was correct. He would come off looking pretty foolish in Willow's eyes if there wasn't a need to rescue anyone tonight. His attention was drawn back to the office by the banging on the door, followed immediately with it flying open, hitting the wall behind it with a crash. "What the hell's going on here?" an angry and drunk Eddie Valcro shouted as he stormed into the room, his face flushed from the exertion of climbing the stairs. His plaid shirt and black pants looked like he'd slept in them. His red hair needed to be cut and looked like someone had tried to comb it with an egg beater.

Melissa swung around a shocked look on her face. "Eddie! What are you doing here?"

"No, the question is, what are you doing with this old man?" Eddie shouted back as he advanced on her like a raging bull.

"What is the meaning of this?" Professor Dinwiddle asked in a voice mixed with shock and anger as he started around the desk towards the intruder. "Who the hell are you?"

"This is going to be good," Willow said in a voice little just barely a whisper.

"Shhh," Val replied, though he had to admit everything was playing out just as he had hoped.

"I'm her boyfriend and your worst nightmare," Eddie replied. As he did so, he shoved Melissa out of the way so he could get to the professor. Melissa staggered back on her heels, lost her balance and fell over, striking her head on the edge of the desk on the way down.

"One down," Willow said, obviously enjoying herself.

"Time to intervene," Val said, reaching down to open the window. It didn't budge. "Shistuon, it's stuck. Help me."

Willow threw him a puzzled look before rushing to his side, and together they pulled on the window frame, slowly raising it. "Some hero you are. Can't even open a window."

Val scowled at her but said nothing, instead, climbing through the opening.

Meanwhile, Eddie and Dinwiddle continued fighting in the middle of the room. Eddie had both hands around Dinwiddle's throat while the older man fought to remove them, rapidly turning blue in the process. As Val straightened up, he glanced at Melissa lying on the floor, moaning softly. As he turned his gaze back to the two men, his eyes fell on the professor's letter opener sitting on the edge of the desk. A thought suddenly occurred to him. Why play the hero and take the chance the professor would simply try to turn on him later? Why not handle the matter for once and all?

He grabbed the opener from the desk and continued walking towards the two struggling men. He glanced back to the window for just a second, long enough to see Willow staring back at him, a slight smile on her face. *I'll show you,* he thought. *I may not be able to open a window by myself, but I can handle an asshole like Dinwiddle when he threatens me.* As he reached the two men, he watched for his opening. Eddie was getting the best of Dinwiddle, whose face was now a bright purplish color, his arms flapping ineffectively against the younger and larger man. Val took a deep breath, raising the blade above his head, preparing to stab it into Dinwiddle's back. As his hand swept downward, at the last second the two men turned abruptly, and the blade entered Eddie's neck just below his head, gutting him like a frog.

The two men fell to the floor in a heap of arms and legs, where they lay with Eddie on top of a mostly unconscious Dinwiddle.

There was a moment of utter silence, broken only by Val's heavy breathing.

"What the fuck!" Willow said as she scurried through the window. "You really did him in, but why the boyfriend?" she asked as she rushed over to Val who stood before the two fallen men, the letter opener still in his hand. "Wait a minute. Do you have a thing for that girl over there? Was this all a set up to get rid of your competition?"

Val shook his head, still dazed by the sudden turn of events. "No, not really. I just..." He paused to catch his breath. "...Missed," he finally added.

"I'll say," Willow replied. "Boy, you did a good job of mucking this up, I must say."

Behind them, they heard Melissa moaning and beginning to stir.

"Yeah, maybe," Val replied. He glanced over to Melissa, who was slowly awakening. "But maybe not so badly that it can't be fixed." He reached into his pocket and pulled out a handkerchief, using it to wipe the handle of the letter opener. He then stooped down to where Eddie and Dinwiddle lay. He reached under Eddie's still, lifeless body until he found Dinwiddle's right arm. He pulled it out from under Eddie and placed the letter opener into the professor's hand, closing the fingers around it.

He straightened up and examined his work. Satisfied, he turned to Willow. "There, that should do it. Now, you get back out on the balcony. Stay there until I call you."

"What are you going to do?" Willow asked, but even as she spoke, she started back to the window.

"Act my way out of this mess," Val replied as she waved her towards the window. "Just watch."

As Willow climbed out of the window, Val looked around the room, trying to visualize what had to happen next. Spying a half-full bottle of water on the desk, he rushed over and picked it up. He walked over to where Melissa lay and stooped down to her side. As he did so, he thought he saw Eddie's body move slightly. Oh shit, don't tell me he's still alive? But in the next moment, he realized it was the professor beginning to move under the dead body. He turned his attention back to Melissa. He poured a little water into his hand and flicked it into her face, then slapped her cheeks briskly.

"Wake up. Wake up, Melissa." He slapped her again and repeated spraying the water on her face.

"What happened?" Melissa asked as she tried to push him away. "Oh, my head."

"I was going to ask you the same thing," Val said as he gently helped her sit up. "I was at a bar a few blocks from here when I heard this guy talking loudly about his girl being preyed upon by her college professor and how he was going to put a stop to it. I thought I recognized him, so I followed him here. As I came up the stairs, I heard this loud bang, and then a bunch of noise like someone was fighting. I ran down here to find these two men lying on the floor next to you."

Melissa looked around the room until her eyes fell on the two men. "Eddie! Oh my God! Eddie!" She tried to get to her feet but fell back over.

"Here, easy," Val said, helping her up. "You must have taken a real conk on the head."

She staggered up and over to her fallen boyfriend. "Oh, Eddie. What did you do?"

The text message. Get his cellphone, Aeo instructed Val.

Where the hell have you been?

Around, Aeo replied noncommittally. *I needed to see how you could handle the situation on your own. I won't always be around to help, you know.*

Val walked over to where the two men lay in a tangled pile of arms and legs. "I'll be. Is that Professor Dinwiddle under there? I think he's still alive." Val moved Eddie's body to one side. As he did so, he reached into his pocket and extracted the cellphone and placed it in his own pocket. He'd take care of it later. "Professor, are you all right?" he asked as he pulled the professor out from under the dead man's body.

"Aargh," Dinwiddle moaned. His hands moved up to his neck, the skin already reddened and bruised. "He tried to kill me," he tried to say, but it came out raspy and garbled. He tried again. "I don't even know who he is." This time the words were more understandable." He glanced around and gasped. "What happened?"

Val pointed down at the letter opener still in the professor's hand. "Looks to me like you killed him, Professor Dinwiddle. I'm afraid I'm going to have to call the police." He reached into his pocket and almost pulled out Eddie's phone, then realizing the error, reached into his other pocket for his phone.

"No, wait," Dinwiddle pleaded as he tried to get to his feet, reaching out to Val to stop him. "Just give me a moment to think."

"Okay," Val replied, "but I must say it doesn't look good. This is your boyfriend, isn't it?" He directed the question to Melissa who nodded. "He obviously found out that the two of you were having an affair and..."

"But we weren't," Melissa shouted and Dinwiddle nodded. Noticing the bottle of water still in Val's hand, he pointed to it. "Please."

Val handed it to him, and he took a couple of long swallows before continuing. "We were just working on a project of mine. I promise it was all completely above board."

Val stared accusingly at the man before replying. "Well, I think given the dead body on the floor there, it'll be pretty hard to convince the authorities that everything was above board. I'm afraid your project, whatever it was, will have to be put on hold for a few years."

"What? Why?" Dinwiddle asked. He tried to stand again and this time was successful, though he staggered and had to steady himself by holding onto the edge of the desk.

"You'll be spending time in prison," Val replied.

"What for? I didn't do anything. At least I don't remember doing it." The pleading tone of Dinwiddle's voice would have pulled at Val's heartstrings if the man hadn't been such an ass about the inconsistencies in his records.

"Okay, I suppose you could use that defense. A good attorney might get a reduced sentence...say three or four years. Of course, good attorneys are costly these days. Yeah, I'd say your life will never be the same after tonight."

Dinwiddle stumbled over to Val. He reached out with an unsteady hand and grasped his arm. "Please, you've got to help me. I can't go to prison. I'm...I'm not the kind of man that could survive in that environment. Help me, please. I'll do whatever I can to make it up to you."

Val paused, pretending to consider the man's plea. He had the professor right where he wanted him. Now, to see just how much he could get out of the man. He glanced over where Melissa still stooped over her old boyfriend's body listening to the conversation. She was in a pretty precarious situation as well. He should be able to leverage the situation to get what he wanted from both of them. Now to close the deal.

"I might be able to help you," Val started, then paused as though considering the situation. "You're both in a lot of hot water though. It won't be easy."

"What did I do?" Melissa asked, suddenly more interested in the conversation. "I was just here helping Professor Dinwiddle on his stupid project."

"Stupid?" Dinwiddle asked.

"Oh, never mind about that," Melissa replied angrily.

"Well, to some, it would look like that you were an accessory to a murder," Val said. "I see prison in your immediate future as well." He watched as her face turned pale. "Of course, your daddy is probably rich enough to hire one of those highfaluting lawyers, but dear ol' daddy will probably never trust his little girl again."

"Shit!" Melissa hissed.

Oops, Val thought. *That's the word I meant to say earlier. Oh, well. There was nothing he could do about it now.*

"Okay, here's the deal," Val said finally, as he looked first a Dinwiddle and then Melissa. "From you," he pointed to the professor, "I need a letter of recommendation. You know, something simple about what an incredible mind I have and how I'd make an extraordinary engineer no matter where I went or what I chose to do." He waited for Dinwiddle to nod before turning to Melissa. "I understand the Oil Baron's Charity Ball is coming up in a couple of weeks."

"Yes, so?" Melissa asked.

"I want to attend. You'll be my date."

"Why would you want to attend such a boring event?" Melissa asked. "Hell, I wasn't going to even go to the damn thing this year."

"That's none of your business," Val replied. "Just make sure we're both on the guest list. I'll pick you up. Be dressed and ready to be your charming self. Who knows, you might even have a good time this year."

"And that's it?" Professor Dinwiddle asked as he leaned against the desk, a relieved look on his face. "We do these things for you, and you'll take care of this mess?"

Val nodded. "Yes, that's it...for now. I may have another request or two down the road, but just get the letter written. I'll pick it up tomorrow."

"And how do you plan to handle this..." Melissa waved her arm. "...Mess?"

"Don't worry about it. The two of you just go home. I'll see to this. Trust me."

Dinwiddle and Melissa looked at each other then shrugged.

"I don't see that we have much choice," Dinwiddle said. "Let's not meet for the remainder of this week. I'll be in touch later."

Melissa nodded. "Fine by me." She stared down at Eddie's body. "He really was a jerk of a boyfriend, but he didn't deserve to die for it. I'll leave first. Wait a few minutes before you go. We don't need to be seen leaving the building at the same time...just in case."

Dinwiddle nodded. "I'll just step down to the men's room and freshen up." He reached a hand up to his bruised throat. "I really thought he was going to kill me."

After the two of them left, Val waited for a minute then motioned for Willow. She opened the window and jumped through it into the room. "You're really quite good," she admitted as she walked over to him and stared at the body. "If you don't make it as an engineer, you should really try becoming an actor. You're a natural."

Val waved off the compliment. "We need to get rid of the body."

"I think what you mean to say is that I need to get rid of the body," Willow corrected him.

"Yeah, I guess so. Can you do it? Make it look like a mugging or something."

"Sure. I have a couple of guys from the neighborhood that could help me. They've no love for the police, but would do just about anything to stay on my good side." Val hesitated. He didn't know if it was a good idea to get anyone else involved. "I can assure you they can be trusted. They're twins, Ted and Ned. They've been competing to get inside my pants ever since they were old enough to know what that meant. It's turned into an innocent game we play. They'll not say a word."

Let her call them, Aeo spoke up again. *We'll need more than one person to do our distasteful tasks. We'll see how these two work out.*

Val finally nodded. "It's your hide if anything goes wrong. Pay them what you think they're worth out of your retainer. I'll reimburse you later."

"Aye, Aye, Captain," Willow replied. Val studied her, trying to make out what she'd said. A moment passed before Aeo interjected. *It's an old nautical term that means she'll do what she's told.*

"Okay, right then." Val walked over to the desk and, using the handkerchief again, picked up the murder weapon where Dinwiddle had dropped it.

"What are you going to do with that?"

"I'm keeping it as a memento of the occasion," he replied as he folded the handkerchief around it. "Just in case ol' Dinwiddle gets any ideas of reneging on the agreement later." He turned towards the window, then stopped. "May as well take the door," he said, turning back around. He hesitated with one had on the doorknob and glanced around the office. Finally, satisfied that he'd covered all the bases, he opened the door and walked out. Upon reaching the ground level, he walked down the street a couple of blocks until he reached a public trash bin. He pulled out Eddie's cell phone, dropped it on the sidewalk and stomped on it before picking it up and dropping it in the receptacle. As he walked away, he started humming an old tune his foster mother, Maude, used to sing while cleaning her house. Those had been good days—simple days. He kinda missed them.

Making Arrangements

Two days after the Eddie incident, Val received a letter in the mail from Professor Dinwiddle. It was a neatly typed recommendation letter on the professor's college letterhead with his signature in bold, black ink. On top was a written message on a yellow sticky note: "Let me know if you need anything else."

That same afternoon he received a text from Melissa:

Arrangements made for the boring ball. Expect invitation in mail any day. BTW, I'll be wearing a lavender gown.

Why in hell should I care what color dress she's wearing, Val muttered as he put away his phone and resumed washing the few dishes left over from lunch. A minute or two later Aeo replied, *I believe she's informing you of that information so you will provide her with a corsage that matches her dress.*

A corsage? What's that?

Flowers, Aeo replied. *Don't worry. I'll contact a florist and order one. You can pick it up on the night of the ball.*

For several days leading up to the ball, Aeo worked with Val to bring him up to speed regarding the customs and mores that were so important around such festive occasions as the Oil Baron's Ball. It all seemed silly and a waste of time to Val, but Aeo insisted. *The Arabian cultures are unique and set in their ways. If you're not aware of them, it could jeopardize the success of our mission. That will never do. So, once again, who are you to meet while at the ball?*

"Sheik Muhammad al-Sinai."

Or...

Or, his daughter, Zillah.

Good. Aeo said. *It is critical that you win them over. Zillah is to become your wife.*

This was the first Val had heard of such an idea, and he caught himself groaning. *Why would I want to marry the daughter of a camel breeder?*

It took a couple of extra seconds before Aeo replied. *I see you've been doing your own research on the internet.*

Val shrugged. *There wasn't anything else to do the other night while I was in the library.*

Well, if you'd spent just a little more time you would have found out that there are very few families of camel breeders in the area any longer. The Sheik and his brothers are some of the wealthiest and therefore the most influential people in the world. Not only do they breed camels, but they also own many oil fields. Marrying into that family will provide you with a great deal of security and privacy, both important to the fulfillment of our prime mission.

Okay, I got it. I suppose this Zillah woman will turn out to be some camel herself, right?

Not at all. I believe most humans would find her a quite respectable choice for a mate. As Aeo spoke, he flashed an image of the woman across Val's mind. *Besides which, in their culture, it's quite acceptable to have more than one woman available to you. It's called a harem. It's not even uncommon for the primary wife to oversee the maintenance of the harem.*

Val shook his head. *I swear the more I learn about the cultures of this world, the more I realize how much better the world will be once we've acquired it.*

Part Three

Ball Night

1

On the night of the Oil Baron's Ball, a sleek, black limousine pulled up in front of Val's apartment. As Val walked out in his newly acquired tuxedo feeling ridiculous in the outfit, a few of his neighbors called to him. "Big night? Taking someone to their high school prom?" Val just waved to them and climbed into the limo.

I don't understand why I have to live in such a small apartment in such a run-down neighborhood if we can afford fancy clothes and cars, Val asked as he looked around at the plush interior, complete with bar and entertainment center.

It's important that we create an illusion of wealth, Aeo replied. *I've managed to hack a small, neighborhood bank in a small southern town, making it look like we've received a small business loan from them, but we're far from flush with money. In fact, both the tux and the limo are rented and will need to go back later tonight.*

Why not just hack a larger bank and open an account with a few million in it?

It's too likely it would be detected and would end up having the authorities coming down on you. Trust me. I'm balancing risk against results.

Val wasn't sure what that last comment meant but decided to drop it.

He arrived at Melissa's sorority house a few minutes later. *The corsage is in the refrigeration unit to your left,* Aeo said as Val started to exit the limo. He circled the car with the flower in hand in time to see Melissa walking down the steps from her house, a few of her friends waving to her from the porch.

"I thought I'd save you the embarrassment of all my friends' teasing," she said, then spun around once to show off her dress. Val had to admit, she looked stunning in her formal gown with the deep scooping neckline and plunging back. Playing the role of human was getting easier. He pinned the corsage to her dress, enjoying the view of her cleavage until he stabbed himself with one of the pins, then focused his attention on the task at hand.

As instructed by Aeo, Val made the necessary comments about her appearance before walking around to open her door. As the chauffeur drove them to the hotel where the ball was being held, Val opened a bottle of champagne for them to enjoy.

"To a most enjoyable evening with a lovely lady," Val said as they clinked glasses.

"Oh, you are such a gentleman," Melissa said in an exaggerated Southern accent. "I'm sure it will be a lovely evening."

"Just remember," Val said, changing abruptly to a business-like tone. "Your job is to be sure I meet Sheik Muhammad al-Sinai and his daughter, Zillah."

"Well, so much for being a gentleman," Melissa replied coldly. "Least I forget myself and my role, right?"

Val took a sip of his champagne before replying. "I'm sorry. It's just that it's paramount that I meet these two people tonight."

Melissa nodded. "Okay, I understand. Don't worry. I'll make sure you meet the Sheik and his daughter." She took a long swallow of champagne draining her glass. "But surely we can mix a little pleasure with our business. Right?" She held out the empty glass so Val could refill it. As she did so, she nuzzled her ample breasts again his shoulder.

Val felt a tightness growing in his groin. "Sure, I guess. I don't see any harm in that." He certainly didn't want this woman working against his plans. By the time they arrived at the hotel, the bottle of champagne was nearly gone, and Val was feeling the first effects of it. He'd make sure to drink only water or ginger ale from here on out, he thought. The last thing he needed was cloudy thinking on such an important night. Still, a little fortification had helped to calm the nerves.

As they entered the expansive ballroom of one of the ritziest hotels in Boston, Val gasped at the sheer number of people before him, all of them dressed in their most expensive attire, the women decked out in the finest jewels, the men all wore tuxes similar to his own. *I bet I'm the only one wearing a rented tux,* he thought.

True, Aeo replied. *You are looking at a collection of some of the wealthiest people in the world. As the USA media like to refer to them, the upper one percent of society. Actually, this group is more like the upper ten percent of the one percent. Go, mingle, have fun.*

Val groaned. Despite having spent days practicing how to act in such sur-roundings, he felt like such a fraud, like everyone could see the rental tag on his clothes. He half expected Professor Dinwiddle to suddenly make an appear-ance on the stage where the full orchestra played and announce that they had an Allacrian visiting tonight pretending to be a human. Still, it was important for him to learn to fit into any and all human societies. No time like the present to practice. He leaned over to Melissa who seemed almost as starstruck as he was. "How about introducing me to your father?"

"Oh, Daddy's not here tonight. He told me that since I was coming, it gave him an out to stay home. He hates these charity events."

A man after my own heart, Val thought.

"But I see several of Daddy's colleagues. I can introduce you to them. Come on." She took Val's hand, and they dove into the crowd of people. For the next hour, Melissa introduced her date to dozens of men and their wives. The names and their position in society spun around in his head. He now regretted the champagne until Aeo piped in. *Don't worry about remembering everything. I'm recording it and already researching them. Just meet as many people as you can, but make sure the Sheik and his daughter are among them.*

Val nodded as he breathed a sigh of relief. He even took two more glasses of champagne from one of the passing trays. He gave one to Melissa and kept one for himself, making sure he only sipped at it lightly. It was nearly eleven o'clock when Melissa nodded towards the far end of the room. "Come with me," she told Val as she took his arm and started guiding them through the crowd. "That's the Sheik and his entourage over there."

As they moved through the other people, Val asked, "Do you see his daugh-ter?"

"Yes, that's her on his left, and if I'm not mistaken, that's her fiancé next to her."

Fiancé? What's that? Val wondered.

Fiancé is a term denoting a man engaged to be married, Aeo replied.

Are you kidding me? What are we going to do about that? Is it permissible for a woman to have more than one husband?

No, not at all. Not even for the daughter of a Sheik. Don't worry about it now. Just meet them.

Melissa waited for the right moment to approached the table, then pulled Val after her.

"Hello, Your Highness. So happy to see you again," Melissa said as she curtsied. "May I introduce my friend, Valentino Hussein. I believe my father may have mentioned we'd be here tonight."

"Yes, yes," Sheik al-Sinai replied. "Good to see you as well. You remember my daughter, Princess Zillah, and my old friend and business associate, Saeed el-Rafiq. They are to be married next summer."

Val bowed to the Sheik and nodded to his daughter. He noticed Zillah checking him out carefully, the smile on her face suggesting she liked what she saw. Why not? Taking a closer look at her fiancé, he was surprised to see that the man was easily thirty years her senior. Was this to be a marriage of convenience? If so, it would be his job to convince her father that it would be far more lucrative for her to marry him. No time like the present to start, he thought.

"It's a pleasure to meet you, Your Highness. I believe you may have received a letter of introduction from one of my professors, Dr. Dinwiddle."

"Yes, I believe I did," the Sheik replied. "I apologize. I didn't make the connection. You're younger than I'd anticipated. I figured one of the most innovative engineers to ever attend MIT would be older."

"Well, Dr. Dinwiddle is most kind for the compliment. He was probably referring to the process that I've developed to refine oil cheaper by some fifteen percent. I imagine it could save your family quite a bit of money over the next ten years."

"Really? Fifteen percent, you say?" The Sheik suddenly appeared more interested in the young American standing before him.

"Yes, and I believe with a little more work, I can increase that to twenty percent."

"Really? Twenty percent, you say?" The Sheik leaned over to his daughter and whispered something in her ear. She whispered something back. While they were conversing in this way, Val took the time to study the princess. She's more attractive in person than the pictures Aeo showed me. Perhaps this will work out okay after all.

He leaned over to Melissa and whispered. "Ask her fiancé to dance."

Melissa shot him a confused look but did as he asked.

As the two left for the dance floor, Val waited for the Sheik to finish his private conversation with his daughter. Zillah watched disinterestedly as her betrothed walk to the dance floor with another woman. Val held out his hand to her. "Perhaps we could join them?" She glanced at her father who nodded. She took his hand. As they strolled towards the dance floor, Val thought, *I sure hope those dance lessons Aeo forced on me pay off.* As the two of them glided across the dance floor to a slow waltz, Val found himself enjoying the experience of holding a woman in his arms. Zillah's soft fragrance of perfume only added to the sensual pleasure of the moment. Yes, he was beginning to enjoy this game of charades indeed.

By the end of the evening and three dances later, Val not only had Zillah's phone number, but he had her promise to put in a good word with her father. She has also hinted to him that she might be staying in the States for a few days on a shopping spree after the rest of her family returned home. "Perhaps we could meet for lunch or a drink," she suggested coyly.

"Most certainly," Val replied. "It would be a pleasure to see you again in a less restricted environment."

Zillah smiled and nodded. "Yes, indeed it would."

All in all, Val deemed the evening a huge success. The only thing standing in the way of their plans was the old man to whom Zillah was engaged. Aeo assured Val that he'd not be an issue. *Old men tend to be accident prone, especially when away from the comforts of their homes. Remember, we now have a team to assist us with such inconveniences.*

━━━━✝╢╟✝━━━━

2

SHEIK MUHAMMAD AL-SINAI hated these charity events even though he realized they were a necessary evil to doing business with Americans. And given the current downward trend of his oil business, he prayed to Allah that something productive would come out of torturing himself in this way. If nothing else, perhaps he would find a way to leverage his daughter's beauty to his advantage. However, the night was growing late so if something didn't happen soon, he would have wasted the evening for nothing.

As he sat pretending to listen to the asinine conversations occurring around him, he noticed a young man approaching with a lady with a large bosom on his arm. She was wearing a lavender dress with a wilted flower on one strap. She looked vaguely familiar, or at least her breasts did. How could anyone forget such gorgeous globes of flesh? Perhaps, if nothing else, he could salvage the evening by enticing her to join his harem.

"Hello, Your Highness. So happy to see you again," the young woman said as she curtsied before him in a way that showed off her breasts further. "May I introduce my friend, Valentino Hussein. I believe my father may have mentioned we'd be here tonight."

Okay, so I'm supposed to know this woman and her father. He racked his brain trying to remember. He recognized the American accent as coming from the south, possibly Texas, but that still left over a dozen people he'd met in the last year.

"Yes, yes," he replied, doing the best he could to fake it. "Good to see you as well. You remember my daughter, Princess Zillah, and my old friend and business associate, Saeed el-Rafiq? They are to be married next summer." *That is if a better offer doesn't come along in the meantime.* But who the hell was this Valentino Hussein fellow, and where had he heard that name before?

"It's a pleasure to meet you, Your Highness. I believe you may have received a letter of introduction from one of my professors, Dr. Dinwiddle."

"Yes, I believe I did," the Sheik replied. *So that's where he'd heard the name, from another idiot Yankee bastard.* "I apologize. I didn't make the connection. You're younger than I'd anticipated. I figured one of the most innovative engineers to ever attend MIT would be older."

"Well, Dr. Dinwiddle is most kind for the compliment. He was probably referring to the process that I've developed to refine oil cheaper by some fifteen percent. I imagine it could save your family quite a bit of money over the next ten years."

"Really? Fifteen percent, you say?" *Was that possible or was this infidel just trying to blow smoke up his ass? Still, he would be a fool not to check it out. If it turned out to be even partly true, it could revitalize his oil business that had been on life support for the past year.* "Yes, and I believe with a little more work, I can increase that to twenty percent."

"Really? Twenty percent, you say?" He leaned over to his daughter who was smiling back at the young man before them. "Find out what you can about this man and his claims."

"Why?"

"Because I said so," he replied. "That is unless you want to end up having to marry that old camel driver beside you, after all." He continued. "If what he says is true, he could be the answer to our prayers—mine for financial salvation and yours from a life laying on your back with a fat old man on top of you."

Normal Life Sucks

James hated to admit it, but the truth was he was bored with his life. Ever since his wife, Jenny, had died of cancer, his life had taken on a drab, same ol, same ol kind of life. Oh, sure, he loved his two daughters, Melissa Jean, who everyone now called Jean, and Jennifer Ann. But lately, Jean's days were taken up by school work and hanging out with her friends. Even little Jennifer Ann had been all but adopted by his sister, Maggie. In the process, Maggie had become the "go-to adult" for both his daughters, leaving James as a parent in name only.

While his HVAC business was doing okay, was even growing with new customers, James was bored fixing and servicing air conditioners and heaters. He and Jersey, his old Army buddy, had met some months ago at the Black Horse restaurant in Bermuda to explore how he might be able to take over Jersey's black-op business, freeing Jersey to purchase the Black Horse and retire on the island. All that was left to do was for Jersey to work out the purchase of the restaurant. That's where everything stalled. The owner of the restaurant wanted far more money than Jersey felt it was worth. Unfortunately, Jersey was stuck on the idea of settling in Bermuda, and there weren't any other restaurants for sale on the island. It was a seller's market at the moment.

So here he was, stuck in limbo, twiddling his thumbs and growing old, and worse—respectable.

He had just about become resigned that his plans with Jersey were no more than a pipe dream when a call came in from Jersey. "Good news! The owner of the Black Horse just had a heart attack and is in ICU," Jersey said without bothering to introduce himself.

"That doesn't sound like good news to me," James replied.

"Ahh, he'll be okay. They got him to the hospital in time," Jersey assured him. "The good news is that he's agreed to a price I can live with so we can proceed with the rest of our plans. I'll be closing on the restaurant by the end of the month. You are still interested in our business deal, right?" James could hear a note of worry creep into Jersey's voice.

"I'll say! If I have to climb under another crawl space to change a filter, I might just have to murder one of my customers. How shall we proceed?"

"Let's plan on meeting at my attorney's office the first of next week. In the meantime, I'll have him put together the documents that'll make the transfer official."

"Sounds good to me," James replied, suddenly excited about his life once again. "Text me his address and the best time to meet. I'll be there."

"Good. Welcome to the world of intrigue and double agents," Jersey said with a chuckle. "I'll see you next week. Any questions in the meantime?"

"Only one. Whatever happened to that soldier that pulled your ass out of the fire in Fallujah? I can't remember his name."

"Oh, that was Sergeant Jacobs," Jersey replied. "I'm afraid he was killed in a helicopter accident. Yeah, it was a tail rotor gear malfunction. Everyone in the copter was killed. Why do you ask?"

"I was just wondering. I thought I might offer him a job once he got out of the service."

"Yeah, he would have made a good addition," Jersey agreed. "I have a few other prospects I've been considering. I'll send you their names, and you can follow-up with them."

"Good deal," James replied. "See you next week." As he disconnected the call, he smiled. Suddenly, life didn't feel at all boring.

He reached for his cellphone again to make a call. "Hello, Maggie? James here. Listen, can you watch the girls for a couple of days. I need to travel down to Fayetteville for some business."

He waited for the inevitable yes. She'd never once said no about anything to do with his daughters. "Great! I'll let them know and remind them to be on their best behavior." They chatted a few more minutes before hanging up the phone. Too bad about Jacobs and the others dying. He would have been a great addition to his new black-ops business. Hmm, he liked the way that sounded.

Dessi Stockton

The last three months had been some of the best Todd could remember. Not since his days back in the North Carolina mountains living with Allan had Todd enjoyed such a peaceful, uncomplicated life. It was easy to figure out why. He loved circus life. Sure, there was plenty of hard work, much of which was repetitive. The tents had to be erected at each new location where the circus would stay on the average five to seven days before moving on which meant the tents then needed to be dismantled. But it was that steady, repetitive, count-on-able routine that Todd enjoyed most.

And, oh yeah, he was also in love with Dessi Stockton. It hadn't taken Dessi long to figure out that the new animal caretaker knew next to nothing about horses, but much to his surprise, she didn't get angry or threaten to report him as a fraud. Instead, she proceeded to give him a crash course in the care and feeding of Arabian horses.

That's how it had started. Before either of them knew what had happened, chemistry had ignited between the two of them. They both started inventing excuses to be in each other's company, much to the disgruntlement of Buzz. That disagreement finally came to a head one night after most of the workers had headed into town for a much needed night off. Shortly after joining the circus, Firefly, who owned his RV, invited Todd to use the second bedroom in exchange for sharing the gas costs. It had worked out well so far. On this night, Firefly had joined the rest of the workers in town. Todd, or Caretaker as everyone called him now, begged off, claiming he had a splitting headache when the truth was he just wanted some time alone.

The circus had been slowly making its way south with the colder weather coming on. They were set up just outside of Tallahassee, Florida. An hour or two after Firefly left for town, Todd heard a knock on the door. He opened it to find an inebriated Buzz standing outside, weaving slightly from side to side.

"Got a sec, Caretaker?" Buzz slurred.

"Sure, I guess," Todd replied. "What can I do for you? Want me to make a pot of coffee?"

"Hell no. It might mess with my buzz," Buzz said, as he slowly climbed the few steps into the RV.

"I'll tell you what you can do though."

"What's that, Buzz?"

"You can keep away from my girl, that's what you can do." Buzz leaned against the kitchen counter to keep from falling.

"Well, now, Buzz, I understand your concern," Todd said, trying to keep from smiling, "but I haven't seen any brand on Ms. Dessi. I think it's up to her who she hangs around with, don't you?"

Buzz blinked a few times, considering the question. "Well, yeah, I suppose, but she's been spending so much time with you that she doesn't even bother to give me the time of day anymore."

"I'm sorry to hear that, Buzz, but she's a liberated and single woman who's going to choose who she wants around her."

Buzz frowned at Todd but didn't say anything at first. Finally, he continued. "I think we need to sort this out as men did in the olden days."

"What? You're not challenging me to a duel are you?"

"Hell, no. Someone could get hurt that way," Buzz replied, then pushed away from the counter. "I am challenging you to an arm wrestling match. Right here, right now."

Todd stared at the smaller man standing in front of him, weaving slightly from side to side. "Really? You want us to arm wrestle for Dessi's attention?

"Yep, the loser...that will be you...will step aside and let the winner...that will be me...win over the fair Dessi's heart."

Todd felt like he'd suddenly been teleported back to the Middle Ages where Sir Buzz had just challenged him to a joust. "Are you sure of this?" he asked.

"It's the only honorable way to resolve this issue," Buzz replied. Strange, he suddenly sounded more sober than he had a few minutes ago. Had his drunk behavior simply been an act? What if it turned out that he was actually the Southeast Arm Wrestling Champion or something to that effect? But as Todd stared at the self-proclaimed rival's arms, he doubted that was the case. While Buzz was in pretty good shape, as were most of the people who worked around the circus, he still would be no match for him. After all, Todd had been working on the more labor intense jobs, like pounding in the large tent stakes, as well as carrying around the large sacks of oats for the horses. "Well, then, here's to honor," Todd said as he waved Buzz to the kitchen table that was kept hinged in an upright position against the far kitchen wall to leave a little more space when not in use.

Now, he lowered it in position and sat down across from Buzz. "Since you called this challenge, why don't you state the rules, so that we're both clear."

"They're very simple," Will replied as he stretched his arms out in front of him, preparing to do battle. "I'll count down from 3. When I say start, we'll both attempt to pull the other one's arm down to the table. The one who succeeds is the winner. The loser agrees to step out of the picture. It would also be helpful if the loser could put in a few good words to Dessi. You know, gently persuade her to give the winner a chance."

"You expect to win this contest, don't you?" Todd asked, impressed by the man's hubris.

"No point in entering battle with a defeatist attitude. Are you ready?" Buzz asked as he placed his right elbow down on the table.

The two men clasped hands and position themselves for maximum leverage; then Buzz started the countdown. "Three...two...one... start." The quick count caught Todd by surprise, and he found his arm forced halfway to the table before he managed to recover. It appeared that Buzz wasn't beyond a little light cheating to gain whatever advantage he could, but it didn't matter. Within seconds, it was apparent to Todd which man had the more significant strength. Still, Buzz had been kind to him, giving him a job at the circus and treating him fairly. So, he allowed the bout to continues for close to five minutes before he finally forced Buzz arm down flat on the table.

"Aargh!" Buzz shouted, then lay his head down on the table as well, exhausted by the effort.

After a few seconds, Todd stood up and patted his opponent on the back. "You battled hard, my friend. I'm sure Dessi would be proud of your effort."

Rubbing his right arm with his other hand, Buzz slowly raised his head from the table. "You'll take good care of her, won't you Caretaker?"

"Of course I will," Todd assured him. "After all, that's my name, isn't it?"

Buzz nodded, then slowly rose from the table.

"How about some of that coffee, now?" Todd asked. He felt sorry for the man. It was apparent the defeat had been a severe blow to his manhood.

"No, no. I've got things to do...like, soak my arm. You are stronger than you look. Have a good evening." With that, he turned and walked out.

Twenty minutes later, there was a second knock on the door, this one much softer than the first.

Todd looked around the RV. Had Buzz left something behind? But when he opened the door, Dessi was standing before him. "I understand you won my heart fair and square. Is that right?"

Todd groaned. "I take it you've been talking to Buzz."

Dessi smiled. "Yes, the poor baby. He was quite crushed, you know. But he did his best to put a good word in for you."

Todd shook his head. "I'm sorry about all this. I didn't know what else to do but humor him."

Dessi shrugged. "Well, are you going to invite me in or not?"

"Of course. I'm sorry, come in." Todd reached out a hand to help her up the stairs, but when he went to release her hand, she didn't let go. Instead, she pulled him into a tight embrace. "Isn't there some saying like, 'to the victor goes the spoils?'" And with that, she reached up and pulled his face down to hers. They kissed for several seconds. "When do you expect Firefly back?"

"Not for several hours. If he's lucky in town, he may not be back before morning."

"Good. I'm sure one of you is going to be lucky tonight," Dessi said as she guided him to the bedroom.

Tying the Knot

1

During his whirlwind courtship of Zillah, Val began to notice Aeo appeared to be pulling back from his usual level of interference. He couldn't say it was unwelcome, only odd. At times, when he expected to hear a comment of a helpful fact or a not so helpful opinion inserted from the artificial intelligence, there would instead be...nothing, only a long pause on occasion as Val waited for the input that never came.

So, it was left up to Val to figure out the process of pursuing his intended victim, except he soon learned that "victim" was not the term to use when conversing with Zillah. Now, instead of having such research conducted by his assistant, Val found himself making his way to the internet. He started spending more time in the library where he found a bank of computers, then decided to buy one for himself, so he could conduct his research at night.

He found the dating process not unpleasant, in large part because he actually found being around Zillah enjoyable. She was not only attractive as human females go but was also intelligent and able to carry on well thought out conversations. It appeared that Aeo had done an admirable job in picking out a mate for him.

For whatever reason that Val could not discern, she also appeared to enjoy being in his company. When their time together was coming to a close, he would suggest they meet again, even the very next evening. She would smile and nod yes, so it wasn't long before Val felt it was time to take the next step in the relationship. Even though they'd been seeing each other less than a month, it was time. After all, there was some urgency in the matter. Zillah mentioned several times that she couldn't stay in the United States that much longer. Her father would finally insist that she return, and if she ignored his command, would likely send his "goons" to bring her home.

Val found the answer to their dilemma late one night when he stumbled upon the idea of eloping. Evidently, such a process of marriage was fairly common, especially in the United States. Besides cutting the courtship process down considerably, eloping would also save a lot of money from the customary wedding process that could be outrageously expensive. Val felt certain the bookkeeper part of Aeo would appreciate the frugal move. The only obstacle Val anticipated he'd have to deal with would be persuading Zillah to go along with it. His research revealed that most young women greatly preferred large and lavish weddings, in fact, insisted upon them most of the time. But to his amazement, when he brought up the idea of their eloping, Zillah readily agreed, was even enthusiastic about the idea.

"You do understand, this will mean only a few of your friends and family will be able to attend," Val said, surprised by her willingness to go along with the idea.

"Exactly," Zillah replied. "Let's do it...tonight. Let's fly to Las Vegas and get married. It'll be so romantic."

"You can do that?" Val said, shocked by her reply. His research hadn't gone that deep. For the first time, he wished Aeo would step in with some helpful advice, but once again there was nothing but silence.

"Come on, Val, where's your sense of adventure and romance? You know your namesake, Rudolph Valentino, would do it."

"You know about him?"

"Sure I do. At least, I do now. I thought your two names didn't match, so I went online and looked Valentino up. You're not the only one that knows how to use the computer. What I don't understand is how much you look like him. How is that possible?"

Val shrugged. How in the hell was he going to explain that? He decided to try one of the techniques Aeo had taught him: deflection. "So, you know I've been doing research as well."

"Of course," Zillah replied. "It's okay. I know my country has many different traditions. I appreciate you trying to adhere to them, but I want you to know they are not that important to me. In fact, I take perverse pleasure in breaking as many of them as I can and watching my father cringe. Eloping with you would give me great pleasure." She leaned over to him and rubbed her body against his. "Not to mention the wedding night itself." She smiled at him.

Val racked his brain trying to figure out what she meant by that last comment, then remembered that many cultures insisted the female refrain from having sex until the wedding night. That had been fine with Val who found the whole area of human sexuality and reproduction a baffling subject. At the same time, on more than one occasion he'd felt his body responding to Zillah's overtures in a strangely pleasurable way, as was the case now.

"Okay, we'll do it," Val finally replied.

"Wonderful," Zillah said. She leaned back away from him so she could pull her cell phone out of her pocket. She flipped it open and started tapping on the keypad.

"What are you doing?" Val asked.

"Making the arrangements," she answered, then held up one of her index fingers of silence. "Hi, Pasha, it's Zillah." After a short pause, "Yes, I know it's late. That's why my daddy pays you such an obscene salary," she said with an edge to her voice. Then, much more pleasantly, she continued, "I want you to book two roundtrip tickets to Las Vegas for the first flight in the morning. Book the return for the following morning." She held the phone away from her mouth for a moment. "I want our first night to be in Vegas." She returned to the call. "Oh, you heard that, did you? Yes, it's true. Val and I are eloping! I know. It's exciting isn't it?" Then, after a long pause, "I don't care what Daddy will say. I know he will be upset, but how could he expect me to marry that fat cow of his?"

She took the phone away from her mouth again, this time covering it with her hand. "It's a game Pasha, and I play. I know she'll now call my father and tell him the news. I'm pretty sure she knows I know. It's like she's a double agent. If I want something to get back to my family, I just tell it to my assistant. It works like a charm."

Val, who was having a hard time keeping up with it all, merely nodded.

"After you book the flight and hotel reservations, I want you to pack a bag for me before you retire. I'll return to the hotel later this evening." She flipped the phone closed, and turned back to Val. "Done," she said as she threw her arms around his neck and gave him a sensuous kiss.

The next morning, the two of them were on a 9:15 a.m. flight to Las Vegas, and by lunchtime, they were married. It had become clear to Val that Aeo's pick for him was a woman of action, but it was just the start of his discoveries that day. Later that night, Val experienced one of the marvelous parts of the human body—the orgasm.

2

"YOU ORDERED ME TO FIND out if Val's claims were true and if so, get them for you," Zillah tried unsuccessfully to keep the anger out of her voice. She took a deep breath, then continued. "Your exact words were, 'do whatever it takes, but get me that formula.' Well, I did better than that. I got you the man who has the formula."

She paused, listening for a moment, then continued. "Yes, I'm sure he's telling the truth. Val is quite brilliant." She paused again. "Yes, I know you expect us to return to live in Dubai. I've already discussed this with Val, and he's agreeable. He is also willing to convert to Islam. He's looking forward to the move and learning more about our culture. I told him about the Falconcity of Wonder real estate development project you're a part of and he was fascinated by the idea. I think, if you give him a chance, the two of you will get along fine. You might even learn to like him." She thought about mentioning Val's idea of building a replica of Falcon Lair, the original Valentino's home in Hollywood, but decided it wiser to save that for a later conversation. Let her father get used to the idea of their marriage first.

"Listen, I need to go. I promised Val I'd meet him for dinner/lunch so we can make final plans. I'll call you again when I have more specifics. In the meantime, relax. Your oil business is about to experience a major turnaround." She paused one last time, then disconnected the line. Not even so much as a thank you from her father for what she'd just done, but really what had she expected? After all, she was only one of his daughters. More of a commodity than a member of the family.

If she were going to find happiness, it would have to be with her new husband, and that was fine with her. It turned out that not only was Val a brilliant engineer, with a little more practice, but he'd also make a pleasing partner in bed as well.

Settling Down

1

By Thanksgiving, the Biddle Circus and Vaudeville Acts had retired to their winter quarters outside of Sarasota, Florida. Todd and Dessi had also become known as the most obnoxiously cute couple anyone in the circus community had ever been around. They didn't care. They even agreed and often played the part to the hilt while on the road. Upon arriving in Sarasota, Todd learned that Dessi owned a small ranch in the area that she'd inherited from her parents several years previously. There she housed the Arabian horses she used in her performance as well as conducting a small breeding program for future performers.

She invited Todd to stay with her through the winter—an invitation which he accepted without hesitation. Neither of them was prepared to talk about where they saw the relationship going, but they also weren't ready to call it off just because the circus season had ended. Todd easily stepped into his role as a hired ranch hand—one with extra privileges which included living in the main house and sharing the owner's bed.

However, during all this, he was reticent to share anything about his life before the circus. At first, Dessi seemed okay with this, but as the weeks and months passed and the two of them became more intimately involved, she began to bring it up more often.

"What does it matter?" Todd asked her one night after dinner while they were enjoyed finishing off a bottle of wine.

"Well, I'd like to know who I'm sleeping with," Dessi replied. "I mean, if I go into a post office, am I likely to find your picture posted on the wall?"

"Nope...well, doubtful," Todd replied, joking with her, but seeing that she didn't think it was funny, he grew serious again. "Listen, my past is boring. I was born, raised to adulthood, ran away to the circus, met the most wonderful woman ever. The end."

"What? No, they live happily ever after?" Dessi quipped.

Well, only if you stop asking me about my past, Todd started to say, but then thought better of it. Such a comment was bound to lead to an argument. He still recalled some nights growing up when he'd hear his dad's and Pat's raised voices through the air vent in his room. He and Dessi had had a few close calls, but so far nothing that he'd call a real fight. He'd just as soon not break that record tonight.

"How about this?" Dessi said after topping off their glasses and finishing off the bottle. "Let's play a little game."

"Like what?" Todd asked. He took the bottle from her. "Maybe Spin the Bottle?"

"No, I was thinking more like Q&A. I'll ask a question, and you answer it. Then you can ask me the same question or a different one. I'll start. Where were you born?"

Todd stared at her for a moment, not sure whether to answer or not. It seemed like an innocent enough question, so he decided there was no harm in playing along. "In a small town in the North Carolina mountains, not far from Asheville."

"Really? I would never have guessed. You don't have much of a Southern accent," Dessi said. "You know, we're slated to do a few shows in that area this coming Spring. Maybe you could drop by and visit your folks."

Not likely, Todd thought but decided it best not to pursue that direction. Instead, he asked, "And how about you? Where were you born?"

"Right here on this ranch," Dessi replied. "Born and raised here. In fact, my mother chose to have a home delivery. I was born in the very same bedroom you, and I sleep in."

"Really?" Now it was Todd's turn to act surprised.

"Yep, the very same. See, isn't this fun? We're finally getting to know each other—that is beyond the bedroom knowing."

"Oh, I didn't know you had any problems with what takes place there?"

"No, not at all," Dessi assured him. "It's just that sometimes I feel like I'm making love to a total stranger."

Todd couldn't figure out how knowing more about a person could improve the act of making love, especially when it was already so good. But then again, there were many things he didn't understand about the opposite sex.

"You've told me a little about your father. At least I know he's a veterinarian. What about your mom. What does she do?"

Oh, no, thought Todd. The game had suddenly dipped into dangerous territory. "She died in childbirth," he said simply.

"Oh, I'm sorry."

Todd shrugged, then stood up. "Game over. How about we open a second bottle of wine?" He walked out of the room without waiting for a reply, vowing never to get trapped into playing Q&A again.

2

LIFE ON THE RANCH MOVED forward through the winter months. Despite meeting with heavy resistance, Dessi slowly peeled away Todd's defenses. He finally told her that he'd been in the military for much of his adult life, though he refused to discuss what had led to his dismissal. She also learned not to try to discuss anything regarding his family back in the North Carolina mountains, not unless she wanted him to close up like a turtle being poked with a stick.

Still, for the most part, the two became almost like an old married couple, comfortable with each other and the daily routine. Todd found ranch life to his liking. He enjoyed taking care of the horses, and there was plenty of hard work that kept him in shape despite Dessi's feeding him three delicious meals a day. He even began to cook as well, though he would never hold a candle to her cooking prowess.

Once evening as the two of them was preparing the evening meal together, Dessi sprung a surprise on him. "What if we didn't go back on the road this Spring? How would you feel about that?"

"What?" Todd asked, turning from the sink where he was drying some dishes left over from the previous meal. "Are you serious?"

"I don't know, maybe," Dessi replied. "I mean, I love it when I'm on the road...once I finally get out there, but when I'm here, I'm pretty content as well. That's been especially true this year."

"Ahh, that's sweet," Todd replied, walking over to hug her.

"I didn't say you had anything to do with it," she joked, "but, yeah, you might have added a little to the contentment."

"What would Buzz and the others say about it?" Todd asked. "I mean, you're the star of the show."

"You trying to top my sweet comment with one of your own?"

"No, really," Todd continued. "Your act is certainly one of the highlights, if not the top one. I've seen you get standing ovations almost every night. What other act can say the same thing?"

Dessi nodded. "Well, you're right that it wouldn't be all that easy for Buzz to find a replacement act, especially this late. Plus, come to think of it, I may tire of you in a few more weeks."

"True," Todd kidded back, "and finding a ranch hand who enjoys the added privileges I receive would be a whole lot easier to find than a replacement act."

"No doubt. Well, as I said, I know once we get back out there, I'll wonder why I ever even brought it up. Still, I may want to plant a seed in Buzz's mind that this could be my last year." She hesitated a moment before continuing. "Look. I don't want to put any pressure on you either. I know this relationship is still pretty new. What I do shouldn't interfere with your plans."

"I understand," Todd replied. "I'm still going to keep an eye out in the local paper for any ads for ranch hands with privileges showing up." He turned around to look at her just in time to be hit in the face by the towel she'd thrown at him.

3

WHEN MARCH ROLLED AROUND, Todd and Dessi packed up all their belongings into the RV. By now the entire circus knew they were now officially a couple, so there was only a little jibbing they received during the first few days. There was more talk about Dessi's newest addition to her act, a beautiful three-year-old gelding by the name of Fahad. Dessi had decided at the last minute to bring him along in the hope that he'd become her best trick pony yet. Todd had his doubts, feeling the horse was just a little too spirited for his taste. But, when it came to horses, he knew better than to question Dessi's judgment. After all, she'd been raised around horses her entire life. Todd was still a newbie horse enthusiast.

The circus troupe headed north, stopping at a few towns in northern Florida and then onto Georgia. Dessi tried to diplomatically let Buzz know that this might be her last season with the circus, but he flat out rejected the idea. "You can't quit now. Not at the height of your career," he pleaded. "Besides, how could we ever replace you? Look, if it's the money, I'll see what I can do with the owners." When Dessi assured him it was not a money issue, he persisted. "Then what is it? Is it Todd? Did he put you up to this?"

Dessi laughed. "You know me better than that. Todd and I did have a wonderful time at the ranch. I won't deny it, but I've been thinking about this for some time. I'm not getting any younger. I'm already twenty-seven..."

"Why that's young," Buzz argued. "You've got plenty of years left in you."

"Okay, okay," Dessi finally relented. "I'm not saying this is for sure. I just wanted to give you a heads up so you could keep your eyes open for a possible replacement."

Buzz looked relieved. "Oh, I'm always looking out for the next great circus act. How do you think I found you?"

"I know, I know. You went to this small rodeo that your friends forced you to attend, never having a clue what you'd find that day." Dessi patted him on the arm. "We've all heard the story a million times. I was even there when you introduced yourself. Remember?"

"Yeah, I remember," Buzz replied a far-off look in his eyes. "I think that's the day I fell in love...with your act, that is," he said, suddenly embarrassed. "It's going to be a great year. Just you wait and see. We've added a few new towns including Asheville, North Carolina, and Louisville, Kentucky."

"Yes, I heard," Dessi replied. "By the way, did you know Todd is from the Asheville area?"

"No, I did not," Buzz admitted. "But then again, I know even less about him than I do most of the other workers. I've never seen anyone more closed-lipped about their past. Makes you wonder sometimes, doesn't it?"

"Tell me about it," Dessi replied. "I'll warn you though. I wouldn't bring up anything about his life in Asheville. It appears to be a sore subject."

"Thanks. I'll keep that in mind. How's it coming along with the new pony?"

"So far, so good," Dessi said. "I think he'll be ready for prime time by the time we reach Greenville, but we'll see. He still is a bit feisty in the ring, especially if there are too many people around."

"Well, don't rush it," Buzz replied. "After all, we want you around for many years to come."

"Yeah, I hear you." She turned to leave. "You take care of yourself, Buzz...and keep your eyes open for that new act."

Mimi and Kendra

Mimi Rawling ran into the dorm room waving an issue of the UNC-A newspaper over her head. "Guess what, roomie?"

Kendra Gardner looked up from the book she was pretending to read while lying on her bed half asleep. "Do I have to guess? I'm so into the history of Mesopotamia that I can hardly hold my eyes open, and now you want me to play a guessing game with you. Really?"

"Oh, never mind. You'd never guess it anyway," Mimi said as she sat down on the edge of the bed next to Kendra, still bouncing with excitement. "The circus is coming to town!" She shouted the news so loudly that Kendra put her hands to her ears.

"Please, use your inside voice," she urged her friend. "Besides, what's all the fuss about? So what if the circus is coming?"

"So what?" Mimi leaned over and grabbed Kendra's shoulders and shook her. "We have to go."

"We do? Who says? Is this a new assignment from your journalism teacher? Another one of those get out into the world and live life assignments?"

"No, silly. I misspoke. We don't have to go, but I want us to go. Come on. It'll be fun. You're all the time studying. Let's take a break. Just a little fun. Pretty please. I'll even pay. It can be my birthday present to you."

"My birthday is still months away, as you well know."

"Well, nothing says we can't celebrate early."

"Isn't a present supposed to be something that the receiver is excited to get, not the giver?"

"Oh, all right. If you don't want to go, I'll see if I can find someone else—you old stick in the mud."

"No, I was only kidding. We'll go. It'll be fun," Kendra replied. "Should we invite Jamie and Sly?"

Mimi thought about it for a moment, then replied. "Nah, I don't think so. Sly and I are kinda on the outs right now. I'm pretty sure we're getting ready to break up."

"Really? How can you tell?"

"Because I'm about to tell him, I need a break, that's how."

"Oh, I see. Well, yeah. Let's just you and I go in that case. When is it anyway?"

"A week from Saturday, unless we want to travel all the way to Greenville to see it a few days earlier. Or maybe we could…"

"Nope. One night of circus shenanigans is more than enough for me. Next Saturday will be soon enough."

"Perfect. I'll get the tickets, and you can pay me back."

"What happened with it being for my birthday?"

"As you said, your birthday is still months away. I just said that to persuade you to go with me," Mimi said, laughing.

"You are the worst roommate ever," Kendra shouted back as she threw a pillow at her. The subsequent pillow fight lasted a good five minutes before the two girls collapsed on their respective beds, exhausted from laughing so much.

The following Saturday, Mimi, and Kendra drove to the fairgrounds across from the Asheville Regional Airport an hour before the show was due to start, despite Kendra insisting that it was way too early.

"I want to get a good seat," Mimi said, "and they're not reserved, so it's first come, first serve."

"All right, all right," Kendra finally said. "But I'm taking a book to read while we wait."

"Boy, what a party pooper. You always have your nose in a book."

"Well, you should be glad I enjoy reading so much. Without readers like me, where would writers like you be?"

Mimi thought about that for a moment, then nodded. "Good point. Take a book with you."

As it turned out, Kendra didn't get the chance to read much. By the time they parked the car and walked to the big top, a sizable crowd had already started to enter. They gave their tickets to a man that had the remarkable resemblance of a shark, then joined the group of families and young students like themselves.

"I sure hope we don't run into Jamie or Sly," Mimi said as they made their way to their seats.

"Oh, that wouldn't be all that bad, would it?"

"It most certainly would. I told Sly I was sick when he called me last night to ask me to a movie."

"Nothing like a circus to prompt a fast cure, I always say," Kendra said. "Are these seats okay?"

"Perfect," Mimi replied. "We'll be able to see everything from here, and we're close enough to the ring, we could almost reach out and touch the performers."

As they sat down, several brightly dressed clowns entered from the far side of the tent, chased by a fire engine full of other clowns.

"Has the show started already?" Mimi asked, glancing at her watch.

"No, I don't think so. They're probably just warming up the crowd." A few minutes later, after the clowns had exited the ring and several of the other performers came out to mingle with the early arrivals, Mimi added, "Aren't you glad we came early now?"

"I suppose, even though I'm not getting much reading done," Kendra conceded. "You know, I've never been to a circus before. This is more fun than I'd anticipated."

"See, what did I tell you? You hang around with me, and the sky's the limit when it comes to fun."

"That's the only reason I do put up with you," Kendra quipped back. "That and your amazing ability to pick up cute guys."

As the stands started to fill up, a man wearing a hat reminiscent of the Cat in the Hat walked around hawking programs. Mimi waved to get his attention and purchased one. As she started leafing through it, she pointed to a picture of a young girl dressed in an outfit of sparkles and spangles. "Oh, look at this." She held it out for Kendra to see. "That's Dessi Stockton. My uncle took me to see her several years ago when she was doing the rodeo circuit. She's fantastic. Looks like she's upgraded to Arabian horses as well."

"You've been to a rodeo as well?" Kendra asked. "Is there anything you haven't done?"

"Oh, yeah," Mimi replied. "If you listen to my journalism professor, I've lived a sheltered life."

"He's wrong. I'm the one who's lived a sheltered life," Kendra replied.

"Yeah, all you've ever done was babysit a young boy who grew at an incredible rate. I wouldn't exactly call that sheltered."

Kendra pursed her lips in thought. "That's true enough." Her gaze took on a faraway look. "I miss TJ. He was a good kid."

"I know. I miss him too but don't talk about him in the past tense like he died or something. He's out there in the world somewhere, no doubt living a very unsheltered life."

"No doubt," Kendra replied, suddenly feeling very sad. "Where are those clowns when you really need them." As she spoke the lights dimmed and a spotlight turned on, focusing on a young man standing in the center of the ring, dressed in a royal blue short coat with tails and black leather boots.

"It's starting!" Mimi exclaimed as she reached over and grasped her friend's hand. "You're going to love this."

Dessi Preps

1

"What's this I hear from Buzz?" Todd shouted as he pulled himself into the RV. "Tell me it isn't true. You're not really planning on riding Fahad for the climatic tricks tonight."

Dessi used the makeup mirror to see him and smiled reassuringly. "He'll be fine. We've been practicing all week."

"Yeah, with maybe three people watching in total," Todd replied, pacing back and forth in the small space. "Have you seen the size of the crowd tonight? It's a sellout, and on top of that they're mostly families with small kids and a bunch of rowdy students."

"That's good to hear. I'm sure Buzz is very pleased. He wasn't sure how well we'd draw in this area."

"That's not the point, and don't try to change the subject," Todd paused in his pacing next to Dessi. He leaned over and turned her around to look at him. "Ride Sharod tonight, like you usually do. Fahad isn't ready. He's too jumpy, especially around a lot of people."

"He's got to learn sometime," Dessi replied. "Sharod is getting older. He needs a second horse that can step in from time to time. Fahad is it."

Todd sat down on the stool next to the makeup table. "Isn't there anything I can say or do to change your mind?"

Dessi pondered the question for a moment before reply. "Nope, not that I can think of." She turned back to the mirror and started applying her makeup again. "Go on now. I have some final prep work to do. Maybe check on the lions to make sure they haven't eaten any of the kids."

Todd sat there for another minute, running his hands through his hair, a feeling of foreboding growing within him. Finally, he sighed. Fahad was a good horse and would do anything for Dessi. He'd come along in his training remarkably well. Surely, everything would be okay. Dessi knew her horses better than anyone. "Okay. I'll go." He looked at Dessi in the mirror. "You look beautiful tonight, like every night with or without makeup."

"And you, dear boy, are a marvelous liar. Now, scoot." She turned around and gave him a quick peck on the cheek, but as she started to turn away, he stopped her. He held her face in his two hands and kissed her warmly on the mouth for several seconds before pulling away. "I love you, Dessi. Stay safe out there."

"Love you too," Dessi replied. "Even though now I'm going to have to reapply my lipstick."

2

FOUR-YEAR-OLD JACKIE Bradley thought a night at the circus was probably the best birthday present he had ever received. He had looked forward to this night despite his older sister's continually reminded him that she'd already been to a circus so this would be her second time. "Stay close to me, and I'll make sure nothing happens to you," she told him as they climbed out of the family's station wagon and started walking towards the biggest tent Jackie had ever seen.

"What are you talking about? What could happen to me?"

"Oh, you know," Justina snapped back. "A lot of circus people are gypsies, and they've been known to steal little boys like you."

"They do not." He turned to his father who was just locking up the car. "Gypsies don't steal children, do they?"

His father frowned and shook his head. "Not likely. Justina, stop filling your brother's head with such horror stories."

Justina smiled, proud that she'd gotten a rise out of both Jackie and her father. Marva Bradley, Jackie's mother, came around the car to join them and the four headed towards the big top. Jackie looked from side to side at the barkers and street vendors who hawked their wares. He knew that since tomorrow would be his birthday, he could probably persuade his folks to buy him at least one thing before they reached the tent, but what? In the next moment, he had his answer when a clown with floppy feet and a painted smile on his face came into view carrying a clump of balloons in every color of the rainbow.

"Can I get one of those, Mommy?" he said pointing to the balloons. "Pleaassee."

He watched closely as his mom caught her husband's attention and received a slight nod. "I guess, but you'll have to make sure it doesn't get in the way of other people seeing what's going on. Can you do that?"

Jackie nodded vigorously even though he didn't have a clue how he'd do what she was asking. "Sure thing, Mommy. I want that red one." He pointed to the largest of the balloons, then watched as his father paid the clown who then handed him the balloon.

"Do you want one, Sis?"

"Don't be silly," Justina answered haughtily. "Balloons are for babies."

"Are not."

"They are so."

"Are not."

"Are..."

"That's enough," Mr. Bradley said. "We're here for a night of family fun, not to argue with each other."

"Are not," Jackie whispered loud enough for his sister to hear without drawing his parents' attention.

As they made their way into the big top, Mr. Bradley looked around at the stands that were already close to capacity. He pointed to an area several yards away. "I think we might be able to squeeze in there. What do you think?"

"You and I maybe, but not the four of us," Marva replied.

Justina pointed to an assortment of children sitting on the ground just outside the ring. "We could sit there with those other kids. I'll make sure Jackie doesn't get into trouble."

Jackie started to tell his folks that he didn't need looking after but then changed his mind, realizing it would be more fun to sit on the ground than in the stands. It would almost be like being in the circus rather than just watching it. He held his breath as he watched as his parents once again communicate silently with each other.

"Okay, fine," he mother said, "but remember what I told you about not letting your balloon block other people's view of the show."

Jackie pulled on the string that the clown had tied around his wrist until the balloon was at his height. He then reached out with both arms and pulled it to his chest. "I'll hold onto it like this," he said.

"Good boy," his mother said. "We'll be right up there if you need anything."

A night at the circus and a red balloon. No question, the best birthday ever.

Fahad

1

Mimi and Kendra enjoyed each circus act as they performed one by one in the center ring, varying from an acrobatic team from the far reaches of Russia, to a high wire act from Japan. They even enjoyed watching as a team of workers set up a round cage and then connected a smaller cage that housed the lions. One of the performers than took charge with a whip and chair and directed the male lions in various tricks while the audience held its collective breath and watched on in amazement. Following each act, the team of clowns danced around to entertain the crowd while the next act was being prepared.

Finally, the highlight of the evening was announced.

"Ladies and gentlemen, please give a warm welcome to Miss Dessi Stockton and her amazing Arabian horses," Buzz announced directing the crowd's attention to the entranceway where a second later, Dessi stormed onto the scene, riding one of her horses. Each horse had been trained in its own set of tricks, so periodically Dessi would exit the ring only to return moments later on the back of another horse. This continued for several minutes, during which the crowd grew louder and more appreciative of the amazing tricks they were witnessing.

Perhaps the most appreciative of all was a small herd of children that had been permitted by their parents to sit just outside the ring to make room for a few more adults to sit in the stands. One small boy of about four years of age, held a balloon in his chubby hands so it wouldn't interfere with the view of the people behind him. Each time a new horse arrived, he would laugh and squeal with delight. Twice he almost lost his grip on the balloon, but each time managed to bring it back under control.

Towards the end of the performance, the lights dimmed, and the spotlight shone on Buzz. "Miss Dessi Stockton will now attempt the most dangerous and death-defying riding trick ever performed in public. Please direct your attention to the center ring as she performs the Suicide Layout on her majestic Arabian horse, Fahad. He waved his arm in the direction of the tent entrance where Farad galloped in with Dessi on his back.

As the horse entered the ring, the crowd applauded and cheered. Farad tossed his head from side to side, very unhappy with the welcome. Dessi reined him in and allowed him to circle the ring in a counter-clockwise direction so he could acclimate himself to the crowd noise. On the second loop around the ring, she waved one arm in the air, then slid off the saddle onto the Fahad's left side where she hung upside down, attached to the saddle with only one leg, her head inches from the ground that whizzed by below her. A wide-eyed Fahad continued galloping around the ring as the crowd cheered.

That's when it happened. As the horse neared the small group of children, little Jackie Bradley let out one of his high pitched squeals when he started to lose his grip on his balloon for the third time. As he clutched at it again, he gripped it a little too tight, and it exploded just as Farad reached that part of the ring. The horse started to rear up while still running at breakneck speed, then tripped, almost falling. As he fought to regain his balance, Dessi's head struck the hard ground with a resounding crunch, knocking her unconscious and snapping her neck.

The crowd gasped, and several of them screamed in surprise by the sudden turn of events. "Oh my God," Mimi shouted, instinctively clutching Kendra's arm. They looked on as two men rushed out to corral the horse who had continued to circle the ring dragging the unconscious and broken body of his rider. As the men fought to bring the horse under control, one of the men slipped a black cloth over the horse's eyes. From the far side of the tent, a third man rushed in. Two of them unfastened the limp form from the saddle while the other one held the horse in check. The third man collected Dessi in his arms and eased her to the ground where he continued to hold her close to his chest.

The crowd looked on in stunned silence as the man buried his head against the woman's neck and shoulder and cried.

"That poor man," Mimi said as she looked on, still clutching Kendra's arm.

"Oh my God!" Kendra exclaimed a moment later. "That man is our TJ!"

⸻ ✹⫔⫕✹ ⸻

2

TODD WAS IN THE PROCESS of storing the metal pieces of the lion's portable enclosure when he heard the shouts from the big top. He dropped the part on the ground and started running towards the main tent; his heart gripped by fear of what he might find. What he saw was even worse than he had imagined. Buzz and one of the clowns were struggling to restrain a riderless Fahad who kept rearing up with nostrils flaring.

Where was Dessi? Todd thought, and an instant later saw her still, distorted body hanging from the other side of the horse. He felt a rush of anguish mixed with anger rising from the bowels of his soul and threatening to explode out the top of his head. Then, he felt a second sensation, even more disturbing. He was beginning to morph into his alien survivalist form. "Nooo!" he screamed to the heavens, forcing his body to stay in its present shape. He stood there for what felt like several minutes but was probably just a few seconds. He took several deep breaths. When he once again felt in control, he rushed over to release her right leg from the saddle strap. As she fell into his arms, he felt the crunching of her neck and knew instantly that she was already dead even though a part of his mind kept denying it. No, no, no. This can't be happening, it said, but his rational, military trained mind knew better. Still, he eased her down to the ground like she was a broken doll that could still be repaired. He stared down at her face, her makeup now smeared with dirt, a nasty scrape on one side at her hairline.

He sat there on the ground, his arms around her still form for several minutes. In the distance, he heard a siren as the EMT ambulance drew near. As it entered the big top, and he heard its doors opening, he leaned over and kissed her on the lips for the last time before easing her down on the ground. There was a flurry of activity around him as the emergency crew leaped into action.

He raised his head. "No need to hurry boys. She's gone." He felt a pair of hands helping him up as someone else looked after Dessi's broken body. The next few minutes were a blur to him. Firefly and Buzz returned to his side after helping to clear the crowd from the big top. He felt Firefly's arm around his shoulders, but otherwise, his body felt numb. Two of the attendants loaded Dessi into the back of the ambulance. As they started to close the doors, Todd stepped forward to climb into the rear with her, but one of the EMTs blocked his way. "Are you her husband or a member of her family?"

"No, just a friend," Todd replied before he realized a little white lie would have been smarter.

"Sorry, only spouses or family members allowed in the back."

Before he could object, Buzz stepped forward. "I'm her boss," he informed the EMT. "I'm also Dessi's power of attorney and emergency contact. She set it up that way in case anything like this ever happened."

So like Dessi to prepare for every contingency, Todd thought.

"Don't worry, Todd. I'll take good care of her," Buzz said, then turned to the EMT. "Let's go."

He stood there in a daze for several minutes with Firefly standing next to him. "Can I do anything?" Firefly asked.

He shook his head. He was about to tell Firefly to leave him alone for a while when he heard a soft voice call out to him,

"TJ?"

He turned to see Kendra Gardner standing at the entrance of the tent with Mimi Rawlings a foot or two behind her. Shark had one arm outstretched in an attempt to keep them from entering.

"It's okay, Shark. You can let them in. They're friends." For some reason he couldn't explain, he could think of no two people he'd rather see at the moment. He stood there in the center of the ring as Kendra and Mimi rushed to encircle him in their arms. He couldn't remember feeling so tired, not since the day he'd fought off the sharks in the middle of the ocean. "It's been a long, hard day," he said as he leaned his head on Kendra's shoulder.

"I know, poor boy. I wish I had a bag of Cheerios for you."

Todd nodded and smiled even though he felt like his heart had shattered into a thousand pieces. Todd could feel the tears run down his face, but he refused to allow even one sob to escape his lips. The three of them stood there for several minutes until Todd finally looked up. "I don't know what to do now."

Kendra and Mimi looked at each other. "There's an Ingle's just up the street that's open all night with a Starbucks inside," Kendra said. "How about we go buy you a box of Cheerios and a cup of coffee. We'll figure it out from there." Todd nodded. "I don't think I can go back to Dessi's RV, not yet anyway." *And maybe not ever,* he thought as the three of them walked out to Kendra's car.

Three Friends

The three friends sat around the table at Starbucks sipping on cups of coffee as they passed a family size box of Cheerios among them. A pair of college coeds strolled by their table on their way to the parking lot. "Did you hear what happened just down the street?" The blonde haired girl asked her friend. "One of the circus performers was killed."

"No kidding," the other girl said, then their conversation faded away.

"Yeah, no kidding," Todd muttered. The three of them sat there for several minutes not feeling the need to talk yet.

Finally, Mimi put down her latte and leaned over towards Todd. "It's so good to see you again after so long. What have you been up to?"

There it was. The question Todd knew was coming and still didn't know how to answer. He wasn't sure how much he wanted to share. After all, Kendra and Mime were two of his best friends. Kendra had been his babysitter for years, and Mimi had helped her homeschool him. During that time he had managed to work up a pretty heavy teenage crush on the redhead. He shrugged, deciding to go with the Reader's Digest condensed version. He briefly told them about his time in the Army, but when he reached the part about his mission to Fallujah, he decided to cut it short. "I decided the Army life wasn't for me, so I got out."

Kendra and Mimi looked at each other for a moment, then Kendra said, "Just like that? I thought you had to stay until they told you to leave or your time was up."

Todd chuckled. "Yeah, you're right, but my time was up, so I just didn't re-up, that's all."

"How did you end up in the circus?" Mimi asked.

Todd shrugged again. "I don't know. A couple of my Army buddies who'd gotten out before me told me about it," he lied. "They were two of the guys back there at the..." He let the sentence drift off. "So, how about you girls," he asked deciding it was best to change the subject.

"Oh, not much," Kendra spoke up first.

"Yeah, nothing as exciting as the Army or running away to the circus," Mimi added. "We're both enrolled at UNC-A."

"Let me guess." Todd pointed to Mimi. "Journalism."

She nodded. "Of course."

He studied Kendra for a moment, not sure what her major might be. "Let's see. How about pre-vet?"

She shook her head. "No way. I've seen how hard Dr. Pritchard works. That's not for me. No, I'm studying psychology, trying to figure out what makes people tick." They all sat there in silence as they all realized there was now a large elephant in the room by the name of Dr. Pritchard. Todd finally tossed several Cheerios into his mouth then asked, "Well, how is he?"

The two girls looked at each other again. "Truth?" Kendra asked.

Todd nodded. "Sure," even though he wasn't sure he was ready to hear the truth.

"He's been better," Kendra answered. She played with a pile of Cheerios on the table in front of her.

"How so?"

"You know that Pat and he broke up, right?"

"No." *Though I'm not surprised to hear it,* Todd thought.

"Well, it was shortly after they split that he fell into a bottle," Kendra said as she glanced over to Mimi.

"Pardon?" Todd asked, a perplexed look on his face.

"Oh, sorry. I mean he started drinking quite a bit. My mom says it's not unusual to smell it on his breath when he comes to the clinic in the morning."

Todd didn't know what to say about that. He'd never known his father to have more than one or two drinks. He sat there munching on the Cheerios, remembering some of the times Kendra and his dad sat around the kitchen table at home with him.

"Why don't you drop in on him," Kendra said.

"Yeah, I'm sure he'd love to see you," Mimi added.

Todd shook his head. "I don't know. When I left, we weren't on very good terms." He realized that was another lie. He and Allan had always gotten along well. It had been Pat that had been a pain in his side, and now she was out of the picture. He looked up to see Kendra and Mimi staring at him, waiting for him to reconsider. "I don't know what I'd say to him, after all this time."

Kendra pushed the box of Cheerios towards him. "Just offer him some of these and see where it goes from there."

Maybe it is time I visited him, Todd thought. There was no way he could stay with the circus now. It would just be too painful. *What was it they said about never being able to go home again? I guess I'll find out if that's true.* For that matter, he wondered if there even was a place he could call home.

Reunited

1

Todd had thought off and on while he was in the Army about reaching out to his dad, but it never seemed like the right time. Now, after the tragic death of Dessi and his near death from the helicopter accident, it was clear to him that he couldn't put it off any longer. He decided it would be best to meet the man he thought of as his father in a quiet public setting. The Esquire Bar & Grill on the edge of Waynesboro on a Saturday morning fit the bill perfectly. He was surprised to learn that the bar was even open for breakfast and even more surprised that the food was pretty good.

As he finished the Esquire breakfast special, sopping up the last remnants of the two eggs over easy with a crust of toast, Todd glanced up to see an older Dr. Allan Pritchard approaching his table, a wide grin on his face.

"Hello TJ," Allan said, as he slid into the bench seat across from him.

"It's Todd now," he replied before dropping the bread into his mouth and washing it down with the tasty coffee.

"Oh, right, sorry," Allan replied. "You've grown up."

"Yeah, and you've grown older."

"Happens to all of us. How have you been?"

"Good enough. And you?"

"Well. The clinic keeps me busy and out of the bars...well, except for today. What have you been up to?"

Todd took another sip of coffee and waited until Allan had placed his order for coffee and a danish before answering.

"In the Army, but I'm afraid that's about all I can tell you about that. You know, national security and all that sort of stuff."

"I was surprised to get your call...but pleased," Allan added.

"Yeah, I thought it was about time we talked. I wanted you to know that I'm doing okay and that I appreciate all that you did for me. I don't know what Pat may have told you about that time back when I ran away..."

"Not much," Allan admitted. "She did finally confess that it was her doing that led to your leaving so suddenly."

"Yeah, well, it seemed like the best course of action for everyone concerned at the time."

"Maybe you're right." Allan waited until the waitress put his coffee and danish in front of him and then departed. "Anyway, that's all water under the bridge at this point."

"Yeah, I guess so. Still, I wanted you to know that I hold no ill feelings about you. In my eyes, you're still the best father anyone like me could hope for."

Allan stared down into his mug of coffee noticeably embarrassed and pleased by the words.

"I also want you to know that I'm not going to mess up your life by trying to re-enter it. That's not what this is about. You have your life, and I have mine. That arrangement seems to be working, so no reason to mess with it."

Allan nodded. "Okay, if that's how you want it."

"It is," Todd replied. "But I do have a few questions I'd like to ask you." He remembered what Pat had told him when she'd given him his fake papers and cut the cord. Now, it was time to find out if she was telling him the truth, or had fabricated the fantastical story that he and Homlin were aliens.

"Sure, fire away."

Todd paused for a moment before continuing. "Where did I come from?" May as well start at the beginning, he thought. He noticed the waitress approaching and waved her away.

Allan looked up from his coffee, a surprised look on his face. "Oh, that," he finally said before taking a sip of his coffee. "Why do you ask?"

"Because it has become clear to me that I'm not like other people, so I want to know why I'm so different." There was no need at this point to reveal any of what Pat had already told him.

"Well, it's a little complicated to explain," Allan began, noticeably uncomfortable by the direction the conversation had suddenly taken.

"I'm in no hurry. Take your time."

"Okay." Allan took a deep breath and slowly let it out. "It started with a late night emergency call. One of my regular clients brought in a stray dog that had adopted them. Her name was Molly, and she was having trouble delivering pups. At least that's what I thought she had inside her at the time..."

Allan recounted the story in detail to Todd who listened without interruption.

"So, I came from one of the larvae you pulled from Molly?" he finally asked.

"That's right."

"Then there was this other man named Homlin. What role did he play in all this, and why was I drawn to him?"

Allan continued to stare down at his now empty coffee mug. "Turns out Homlin was the one who'd implanted the larvae into Molly and other animals. It was all part of his plan to take over the world."

"Really?" Todd replied. "But why? How?"

"Well, you see, Homlin wasn't exactly human. In fact, he wasn't human at all. No one really knows where he came from, but it is clear it wasn't from this planet."

"So, Homlin was an alien?" Todd asked.

"Yes, that's correct."

So, Pat had been telling him the truth. How about that. "And I came from Homlin...whatever his mission was..." Todd paused for a moment, thinking through the conversation. "So, that makes me an alien."

"Well..." Allan started.

"No, no. No need to sugar coat this or try to explain it away," Todd interrupted him. "You know what they say. The truth will set you free."

"But first it'll piss you off," Allan added.

"Not in this case. I'm going to skip that step if it's all the same to you. I feel quite free knowing this. I've felt like I came from another planet most of my life. As hard as it is to believe, it's good to know that it's actually true."

The two men sat staring at each other for over a minute. Finally, Allan leaned over and took Todd's hand that was resting on the table next to his cup of coffee.

"There's one more thing I want to tell you, and I ask that you take it to heart. Consider it my last life lesson, at least for now."

Todd nodded. He looked down at their two hands, surprised how natural and good the contact felt. Allan had never been a very touchy, feely kind of father, but now and then he'd reach out and pat him on the back, or mess up his hair. Todd now realized how special those small moments had been. This felt like one of those moments.

"How and where you were born is part of your past. Sure, it's part of your heritage, but it doesn't have to predetermine the rest of your life." Allan paused as though trying to think out what he wanted to say next. "You know people who aren't born in this country but come here later from another part of the world are considered to be foreigners. Right?"

"Yeah, I guess. Sure."

"But eventually many of them decide that being a foreigner doesn't work for them anymore, so they go through a process to become American citizens."

"Right," Todd said, unsure where Allan was going with this.

"So, what's the difference between being a foreigner or an alien except maybe the distance? You did the work to become an American soldier. You've worked hard to fit in, not only in this country but the world...the world of humans. So, as far as I'm concerned, your being alien is a moot point. It's the point I could never get Pat to understand."

Todd nodded, finally getting the point.

"No matter what happens from here, no matter how bizarre or alien your origin, you're my son...my human son, and I love you in that way," Allan said as he squeezed Todd's hand.

Todd looked up at his father and was surprised to see tears in the man's eyes; then he realized his own eyes had teared up as well. He coughed to clear his throat from the sudden tightness. "And you are my dad that I will always love. I'll do my best to make you proud."

2

THE TWO MEN CONTINUED to sit across from each other enjoying each other's company over another cup of coffee. Finally, Allan asked, "What's next for you?"

Todd shrugged, realizing it was becoming a natural response to such questions.

"I'm not sure. I think I told you on the phone; I ran into Kendra and Mimi the other day. They were the ones who suggested...well, more like ordered me to come see you." He thought about telling his dad about his circus experience and life with Dessi but then thought better of it. That wound was still too raw to scratch. "They invited me to come visit them in Asheville. I thought I might do that. Beyond that, I'm not sure. Just taking it one day at a time right now."

Allan nodded. "Sometimes that's the best way to approach life. Hey, do you need a little cash?" He started to reach into his back pocket for his wallet.

Todd held up his hand. "No thanks, Dad. That won't be necessary."

"You sure?"

Todd nodded.

"Well, be sure to tell the girls hi for me."

Todd nodded again. "Listen, Kendra told me she and her mom were a bit concerned about your drinking..." His voice trailed off.

It was Allan's turn to nod. "They're right to be concerned, but I can assure you it won't be a problem any longer."

"How so?" Todd asked.

"Because I want you to be proud of me as well."

Todd smiled at this response. Funny, he'd never thought that pride could go in both directions.

"You know, if you wanted, you could come home and spend the night," Allan said. "For that matter, you could stay as long as you'd like."

Todd considered the invitation. He'd had some good times there, but there'd also been some bad memories created there—more than he'd care to dredge up at this point. He shook his head. "Thanks, but I think I'll just head on to Asheville if it's all the same to you."

Allan seemed to accept his decision fairly well. "Okay, well, at least let me drive you to Asheville."

"Oh, no, that's way out of your way. I'll be fine."

"Really? How you plan to get there then?" Allan asked. Todd held out his thumb. "No way, I'm driving you, and that's final," but Allan smiled to soften the words. "Just pretend you held out your thumb, and I was the one that picked you up."

"Okay, I guess I can do that."

The two of them got ready to leave. Once again, Allan insisted on picking up the tab. "It's the least I can do after what Pat and I put you through," he said.

Todd started to point out that it had really been Pat that had made those times so difficult, then thought better of it. *Let it go,* he told himself.

The drive from Waynesboro was quiet with neither of them knowing quite what was safe to discuss, so they mostly listened to the music on the radio. The station was honoring a local folk singer by the name of Amberlin by playing her top hits that had been popular back in the sixties. Todd had to admit she had an angelic voice. No wonder she'd been so popular.

"Do you want me to drop you off at UNC-A?" Allan asked as they entered the Asheville city limits.

"If you don't mind, how about dropping me off at Park Place. It's a nice day, and I'd like to walk around for a bit."

"You've got it."

When they arrived at the public park that had been Todd's hangout after he'd run away from home, Allan pulled over to the curb to let him out. Todd turned to offer him a hand. Allan took it then pulled his son to him in a hug. "You take care of yourself, son. Remember, it's a dangerous world out there."

You're telling me, Todd thought but instead said, "I will, Dad."

Back to Asheville

1

The spring-like weather had brought out an eclectic crowd of people to Pack Square Park including college students, elderly couples, and a higher percentage of hippies than you'd likely see in any other city, at least on the east coast. As Todd walked around, he remembered the many cold nights he'd spent in the area, more than a few of them sleeping in a dumpster that had served as his only shelter in those first days in Asheville. It's a wonder I survived those times, he thought, then realized he could say the same for much of his life. He wasn't sure why he'd asked Allan to drop him off at the park, but it felt good to return to his old stomping grounds. Sure, there'd been some harsh conditions, but there'd also been some good times as the homeless population of Asheville had taken in a young boy who didn't have a clue how to survive on his own, but with their help, he'd done all right. He thought back to some of his homeless friends: Peggy Sue, Elmer Fudd (turned out it had been his real name), and Alley Cat, the cute one with the large boyfriend. Of course, not everyone on the street became his friend. Saul and Sally had been particularly bad apples and had almost gotten him arrested by Big Blue, the street name for the police.

As Todd strolled around the park, he was disappointed he didn't see anyone he knew, but he supposed that was understandable. His friends had all been homeless after all, which meant they didn't maintain deep roots in any one area. Suddenly, at the far end of the park, he saw an old man sitting cross-legged on the ground wearing a faded green Army jacket. Luke! That's why he'd come to the park. Luke, the old Army veteran, and his dog, Precious, had been his two closest friends. It had been Luke who had gently—well, maybe not so gently—guided him into the Army. While it hadn't ultimately turned out so well, he realized he once again needed to tap into his old friend's wisdom.

But as he ran towards the man in the Army coat, something didn't feel right. He'd always had the knack of sensing when people he knew were around him, but he had no such reading this time. As he drew closer, he realized the man wasn't his friend, after all. As he slowed his pace to a walk, the homeless man looked up at him, a scowl on his face. Todd reached into his pocket and dropped a handful of coins into the man's tin before continuing. It appeared that even Luke had headed on to greener pastures. He glanced at his watch. It was about time he headed towards UNC-A's campus anyway.

2

ON A DISTANT KNOLL overlooking the park, a man in a faded green jacket lowered the monocular from his eye and placed it in his coat pocket. He pulled out a phone, and after tapping in a number, waited for someone to pick up on the other end. "I thought you told me Sargeant Jacobs had been killed in a helicopter accident last year?" He listened for a moment before continuing. "Then how come he's walking around Pack Square Park as though he was alive? No, I'm not shitting you. I'm looking at him as we speak." He paused again to listen. "No, I won't say a word to him. That's why I called you first." Pause. "Yes, I'll keep an eye on him until you get back in touch with me." He flipped the cell phone closed and turned to call to Precious before realizing for probably the twentieth time that the Cocker spaniel was no longer with him. The memory of his old companion still hurt his heart. He sighed, then started following the young man that he'd thought was dead.

3

TODD TOOK HIS TIME walking the two miles to the UNC-A campus, stopping from time to time to take in the sights and enjoy the crisp, clean air of Spring. He arrived at the girl's dormitory a little after two and asked the attendant behind the desk to call up to them. He waited in the lounge downstairs as several coeds walked through to check out the "hot hunk." He smiled pleasantly at them but made it a point not to encourage anything further. It had been just over a week since Dessi's fatal accident. He'd spoken to Firefly a couple of times as well as calling Buzz to let him know that he'd not be returning to the circus, Todd knew it would be a long time before he'd be interested in getting involved with another woman, if ever.

Mimi and Kendra arrived within a few minutes, and the three of them walked to a nearby coffee house. They sat outside on the patio enjoying their various coffee brew. "How did it go with Allan?" Kendra asked.

Todd nodded his head as he pondered the question. "Good," he replied. "It was good to see him again, and I think he enjoyed it as well." There was a long pause.

"And?" Kendra prompted him.

"And he promised to lay off the booze," Todd added.

After another pause, Kendra asked, "And?"

"That's pretty much it," Todd answered. Kendra and Mimi looked disappointed, so he finally added. "It's not quite true what they say about never being able to go home again. You can go home. You just can't stay, not for long. At least I can't if that's what you were wondering. It's time I moved on."

Kendra and Mimi looked at each other. Finally, Mimi asked, "To what?"

"Pardon?"

"Move on to what?" Mimi repeated.

There it was. The question he had been avoiding asking himself. After all, he was dead to the rest of the world, and he definitely wasn't interested in coming back to life as Sergeant Todd. He'd probably be arrested for going AWOL or something worse. No, he'd just as soon stay dead. So, here he was, right back where he'd started when he had run away—homeless in Asheville. Well, that wasn't entirely true. His survival skills had definitely improved. Something would turn up. It always did.

After a few more minutes of chatting, Todd stood up. "Listen, I've got to go meet a man about a dog..." Funny, he'd not heard that phrase for years, since he'd lived with Allan who'd used it on occasion when he had to go somewhere but didn't want his young son to know where. "I'll be in touch."

The two girls, who looked shocked by his sudden decision to leave, stood up to give him a parting hug goodbye. He walked through the coffee shop and out onto the street. He looked to his right and then his left. Since he'd arrived from the left, he decided turned to the right. He'd walked only a couple of blocks when he started to feel the presence of someone he'd met before. Was he being followed? As he stopped at the crosswalk waiting for the light to change, he glanced over his shoulder. Sure enough, a man in a faded green Army coat strolled towards him. This time it was his old friend, Luke, but without any sign of Precious.

The two shook hands which progressed into a bro-hug. "You're looking well," Luke said, then added, "especially for a dead man."

"How did you hear about that?" Todd asked.

"I have my ways," Luke replied. "Listen, I have someone I want you to meet."

Todd nodded. "Okay, I guess, but why?"

"He might have a job for you. In fact, he might have several jobs."

Todd thought about that for a moment. "Okay, sounds good to me. Let's go." The something had apparently turned up.

Meeting

Luke hailed a cab, and as the two of them climbed in, he gave the cabbie an address that Todd didn't recognize. As they drove through the streets of Asheville, the buildings grew older and shabbier until they finally arrived at a section of town that appeared made up of mostly abandoned stores and warehouses. Todd wondered what Luke was up to but decided to keep his mouth shut and see how it played out. After all, Luke was one of those few friends who he trusted completely and had never led him astray. Of course, that had been the Luke he had known from years ago, and sometimes people change and not always for the better.

As the cab pulled into the location Luke had provided, the old Army veteran paid the driver. The two men exited the cab, and it drove off, leaving them alone on the street in front of an abandoned warehouse with a tilted sign that read Swift's Meat Packing Company. Todd raised an eyebrow but remained silent.

"We'll go in the back way," Luke instructed pointing to an alleyway.

"Fine by me," Todd replied. "Wouldn't want any of my friends to see me frequenting such a plush location."

Luke smiled but remained silent.

As they walked down the alleyway, the bright sunlight gave way to dark and foreboding shadows. Todd eyes quickly adjusted to the change as did his hearing and other senses. He felt another presence of someone he knew besides Luke. The sensation was not as strong as it had been for his old friend, which suggested that whoever he was about to meet was probably just an acquaintance, someone he'd met in passing and might not even recognize this time around.

Approaching the back door of the warehouse, Luke pulled a key out of his pocket, unlocked and opened the door. He stepped aside and waved Todd to enter the darkened abyss. *People change and not always for the better,* he thought again, as he went into the building.   ·

"To your left," Luke said. "Head towards the light down there."

Todd followed his direction, a feeling of foreboding escalating as did the sensation of familiarity. The light was coming from a partially open door at the end of the hallway. Todd stopped outside the door to glance at Luke, who waved him forward. "After you. I'll make the introductions; then I'll be heading out."

Heading out? How was he going to get himself back to civilization? Todd wondered. He regretted for not the first time not purchasing a burner phone, but it was too late to do anything about it now. He pushed the door the rest of the way open and walked in.

A large man wearing a cream colored shirt and blue jeans sat behind a makeshift desk. The only light came from a desk lamp that kept most of the man's face in shadow. "Good to see you again. I'm happy to learn that the re-ports of your death were greatly exaggerated." The man pointed to a chair across from him. "Have a seat." He looked over at Luke, who continued to stand in the doorway. "Much obliged. I'll take it from here." Luke nodded, then gave Todd an informal salute. "Don't worry. You're in good hands. He'll treat you right." And with that, he disappeared they way they'd come, closing the door after him.

"We've met before?" It was as much a question as a statement. The man looked vaguely familiar and yet felt even more familiar. Where had their paths crossed? The man's force had a note of authority like he was used to having his requests honored. That suggested military. That would match with the little he knew about Luke's past as well. Then it came to him where they'd met—on the mission outside Fallujah. "You were one of the pilots on that Fallujah mission, weren't you?"

The man nodded. "And you're the soldier that salvaged that clusterfuck of a mission, and in the process, saved the life of my friend, Jersey." He stood up, leaned over the desk to offer his hand. "Name is James," he said as they shook hands. He sat back down placing himself back in the shadows, but for that brief moment, Todd had a good look at his face and memories of that night rushed in. One more time he'd almost been killed.

"You seem to have a knack for getting out of tight spots, don't you?" James asked.

"Well, I guess I'm just lucky," Todd replied.

"That may be part of it." James leaned back in his chair and placed his hand behind his head. "How would you explain surviving that helicopter accident off the coast of the Carolinas? You know, the one where everyone else died and that you were reported to have been killed as well?"

What the hell was going on here? Had Luke set him up after all? Was a couple of MPs about to walk through the door and arrest him for going AWOL?

"Relax," James said. "As far as I'm concerned, you died in that accident. I see no need to set the record straight. I'm just curious how you managed to escape."

Todd shrugged. "It wasn't easy, but as I said, I'm lucky."

"Okay. Fair enough," James said. He leaned forward in his chair, placing his elbows on the desk in front of him. "I find in my line of work there are times I could use a lucky guy on my team. You interested?"

"That's hard to say," Todd replied. "Depends on what your line of work is."

"Black ops," James said. "Sometimes the contract is from the United States government, sometimes not, but basically you'd be a modern day mercenary, a soldier of fortune, not all that different from Chris Jacobs' profession."

Holy shit, where had he come up with that name? Chris Jacobs had been the fictional character in the video game Todd had played growing up. This dude must have done his research.

"Interested?"

"I could be persuaded," Todd replied.

Epilogue

It was hard for Dr. Lionel Adams to believe it had already been a little over three years since he'd joined the biogenetic research team of Bio Vita Tech, one of the most prestigious companies in the Research Triangle Park of North Carolina. The Triangle, as it was commonly called, housed over two hundred companies which employed over 50,000 people, some of them the most prominent scientists and technicians in their field. It had felt like such an honor when BVT offered him a position. He was even more blown away by the salary they offered, which was above anything he'd ever dreamed of making. As a young nerd breeding rabbits and growing various strains of peas to teach himself genetics, this was a dream job.

But now he was wondering how much longer he could count on BVT's support, especially from the head of the facility, Franklin Pruitt. For the past three years, his entire life had focused around one primary aim: how to tap into the full potential of the human mind. During that time he'd carried on his internal debate. Would succeeding at this lofty mission be a brilliant breakthrough for science, or would it turn out to be one of the worst ideas in the history of humankind? Despite that unanswerable question continually gnawing at the corners of his mind, Lionel had averaged over sixty hours a week in his lab trying to crack the code on human potential.

Sure, he'd made some exciting progress, a few that bordered on breakthrough research themselves. This had been especially true after receiving a strange package from a college buddy of his that held frozen larva of unknown origin encased in dry ice. He still didn't know why Dr. Allan Pritchard had mailed the specimen to him, and a phone call to the small animal veterinarian had proved unhelpful as well. About the only thing he learned from the conversation was that the specimen was "not of this world," whatever in the world that meant.

Nevertheless, it had proven instrumental in his genetic engineering re-search. It had, in fact, been key to most, if not all the minor breakthroughs of the last three years—those results that kept BVT funding his research, despite the quarterly meetings he and Franklin now had to discuss how much longer they were likely to continue pouring money into the black hole.

He had to admit it was a strange combination that had led to the line of research he was now pursuing. Who would have thought that a rare species of blue-green algae combined with an unidentified frozen larva from "out of this world" could produce, well, for instance, a species of rodents with enough legs to resemble a centipede? Or a guinea pig with a whistle that could shatter glass. Of course, neither of those results were marketable in any shape or form. And as Franklin reminded him almost every meeting, "while BVT is a research fa-cility, we owe it to our stockholder to occasionally show a profit, which means some of the research must lead to useful and profitable products." Franklin had not been amused when Lionel had tried to convince him that the multi-legged rodents might prove to be the next Pet Rock craze. He had made a good point that along with the extra legs the rodents had a vicious disposition and would have eagerly eaten any child who received one as a present. "We're fighting off enough lawsuits without adding those to the mix," Franklin said, nixing the idea.

So, here he sat in one of the most well equipped genetic labs in the country, if not the world, trying not to dwell on the many failures while the unanswer-able question reverberated in the background of his mind: would unlocking the human potential be a scientific breakthrough or a really bad idea? Hell, it was a Friday night. He should have accepted the invitation from the cute blonde technician to join her and some of her friends for drinks at the Rathskeller. It wasn't like he didn't enjoy a good time, but the truth of the matter was he wasn't comfortable around attractive women, and El Cutie was definitely attractive, as were all her friends. But it was even worse than that. Women scared him, always had, probably always would. It wasn't like he hadn't tried to overcome his fear. He'd read books on the subject. He even tried some of the exercises in the back of each chapter. They had helped, kinda. Now, when cornered by a woman at a mandatory company party, he could carry on a conversation. That is if asking the woman what she most enjoyed about her life and then listening attentively counted. But beyond that, he was pretty much stuck in the early teenage adolescent mode when it came to women.

He glanced at his watch and was surprised to see it was already after ten p. m. His brain was too fried at this point for anything productive to come out of the evening. He might as well head on home and get a good night of sleep. Maybe, he'd stopped by the community church. Of course, no one would be there this late at night, but that's how he preferred it. The church had an open door policy which included keeping their main sanctuary open 24-7. He still didn't know whether he believed in a God or not, but he had to admit, God's house did provide a quiet setting where he could unwind after a hard day of making little if any progress. He shut off the lights and most of the equipment. Maybe tomorrow would be the day when the next big breakthrough happened. It was that same thought that had kept him going for these last three years and would need to sustain him for a while longer.

End of Book Three

Next--*FreeForm: New Birth*

Enjoy this sample chapter of

FreeForm: New Birth
Room 707

707. This is the room, Flip MacDougal thought as he glanced up and down the hallway. The institutional gray walls and black and white checkerboard floor made him feel like he had stepped into a black and white television show from the forties. If his information was correct, Dr. Lionel Adams, one of the most prominent genetic researchers in the world, worked on the other side of the door. It had been so easy up to this point to gain entrance to the lab. Denise, his seductively attractive connection was right when she'd told him breaking into Bio-Vita would be a piece of cake.

Flip tried to imagine the look of astonishment that would be on the doctor's face, finally deciding it was easier to see it in person. He adjusted the mirrored sunglasses, then moved the attache case from his right hand to his left so he could take the black enameled card from his trench coat pocket, an essential item provided by Denise. Within the thin layers of plastic, resided the magnetic code to this as well as other doors throughout the research facility. He placed the card in front of the screen of the security lock so it could read the holographic image imprinted on the card. The latch silently tumbled open, and a thin ray of light appeared at the edge of the door. Flip pushed it open and walked into the lab.

Across the room, a lone figure sat on a wooden stool, his back hunched over a binocular microscope. The white lab jacket, draped over angular shoulders, was motionless, its wearer intensely concentrating on the scope. Flip stepped lightly across the room, his Reeboks muffling the footsteps as though someone had cut the sound on the television. He stood behind the scientist, reveling in the triumph of the moment. Flip lowered the attaché case to the floor, careful not to disturb the silence. His gloved hand released the handle and slowly joined its partner. The two hands traveled steadily towards the hunched shoulders. As though on cue, Lionel raised his head away from the microscope. Perhaps a premonitory warning had finally knifed its way into his consciousness. The hands continued towards the neck, paused, and then moved again, not to the neck but toward the eyes. The smooth leather caressed the eyes, closing off all light. "Guess who?" Flip asked, his soft voice shattering the silence like an alarm.

Lionel Adams sat in front of the microscope, entranced by the sight of the mutated cells, slowly becoming aware of a sharp pain in his lower back, a product of sitting too long in the same position. It's amazing, he thought, how those tiny flagellated cells could be such an important part of the creation of life. He continued to watch, hoping to find at least one altered in some way. Perhaps it would move a little faster or have a more direct path across the slide; anything that would suggest a change in the cell.

Only the twitch on his nose was finally able to break his concentration. Sneezing while looking in a microscope can be devastating on your sight, he thought as he looked up for a moment and sniffed in an attempt to hold back the sneeze. Still concentrating, now on the sneeze, the sudden loss of vision followed immediately by a strange voice behind him sent Lionel leaping off of the lab stool. While still in the air, he twisted in an attempt to see who was behind him.

"What the...who the..." He gasped as he fought to regain his balance. The intruder stumbled back, laughing hysterically, and tripped on something behind him.

"Oh, God...did I ever get you...Oh, what an expression..."

Lionel finally found his balance, coming to rest against the counter, his hands grasping it for support. Glaring harshly at the intruder, he tried unsuccessfully to see through the man's disguise.

"Don't you recognize me?" The stranger asked as he pulled first one glove, then the other, from his hands. Then removing a pair of sunglasses, he placed all three items in his coat pocket. "Your lifelong friend and fraternity brother?"

"Flip? Flip MacDougal?" Lionel stared unbelievingly at the man, unconvinced his old friend could possibly be in his secure, top-secret lab. He slowly recognized the truth. "Flip, can it be...yes, it can. Flip, I swear, I'll strangle you with my bare hands this time."

Still weakened from laughing so hard, Flip circled away from his friend.

"Now Lionel, control yourself. Remember, you're a respected scientist and community leader, or something like that." The two men circled around the stool, exchanging places.

"I swear, Flip, you've outdone yourself this time. If I weren't so glad to see you, your life wouldn't be worth diddly right now. As it is, you still deserve a thorough thrashing." Lionel continued to stalk his old friend but stopped suddenly as he noticed Flip's hand glide across the lab counter. As though in slow motion, he watched as it collided with the glass beaker half-filled with an aquamarine colored reagent.

"Watch out..." he began but knew it was too late. "Don't get it..." but stopped again, realizing the second warning was also too late as the beaker tipped over, spilling its contents across the counter.

"Damn. Sorry about that, Lionel. I hope it wasn't something important." Flip looked around frantically for something to wipe up the spilled liquid. Spying a box of Kimwipes, he yanked several tissues out of the box.

"No, don't do that," Lionel shouted as he grabbed Flip's wrist, inches from the pooled liquid. "Let me clean this up. Go down the hall and wash your hands thoroughly. Use plenty of soap. I'd let you do it here, but I don't keep soap in the lab."

"No problem." Flip said as he started to wipe his hand on the trench coat then stopped, a look of concern on his face. "Is it acid or something?"

"No, it's...it's just best you get it off your hand as soon as you can, that's all. Now go. I'll clean this up." Lionel reached into his pocket and pulled out his ID badge. "Here, take this in case someone stops you. Tell them you're assigned to this lab."

"No problem, Li. You know, I can always talk my way out of anything. I need to bleed the old snake, anyway."

"I'm beginning to remember," Lionel replied. He watched until the door closed behind his friend, then quickly grasped a small glass pipette and bulb and began carefully sucking the liquid back into the beaker.

Flip pushed the door to the men's room open, and with each passing minute was less concerned about the fluid remaining on his hand having any adverse effect. With nature calling with increasing urgency, he walked to the nearest urinal and, without bothering to untie his coat, raised its hem and unzipped his pants.

"Ah, the pause that refreshes," he muttered as he stepped a little closer to the urinal. As he finished, he noticed a small pubic hair sticking tenaciously to the tip of his penis. Without thinking, he picked at the hair to remove it. As he did so, he felt a stinging at the tip of his penis and realized he'd used the contaminated hand.

"Shit," he muttered as he quickly shook his penis and returned it to his pants. "I better wash this stuff off before it starts to eat my hand off."

But the damage had already been done. Microscopically, the complex compound from his hand mixed with the fluids of Flip's organ. Molecule after complex molecule traveled up the urethra. The journey was a slow one, but there was plenty of time. The journey would be complete, and the near magical molecules would be well seated in the testicular tissue of Flip's sexual organ long before there would be call for him to flush the biological tube again. By then, it would be too late. By then, the seeds of a new birth would have formed in Flip's loins.

"Important?" Lionel muttered as he worked to save as much of the precious fluid as possible. "Nine months of distillation to get this much template and it took Flip less than that many seconds to jeopardize my entire project." He shook his head, but a smile crept on his face. He had to admit it was good to see the old bastard again.

Lionel had finished rinsing and collecting the fluid for re-distillation when Flip returned to the lab. Before Flip had a chance to speak, Lionel said, "Don't bother asking me about it, Flip. You know I can't tell you what I'm doing here, but you damn sure better tell me what you're doing here; more importantly, how did you get in?"

After inspecting the nearby counter to be sure it was clear of any glassware, Flip pushed himself onto it. "It was quite simple, Lionel, but before I tell you, do you promise not to report it to anyone?"

"You know I wouldn't do anything to get you into trouble."

"It's not me I'm concerned with. Promise?"

"Sure."

"Well, you know the lady who sits at the front door?"

"Yeah," Lionel replied slowly, a look of recognition appearing on his face. "You mean Denise?"

"Yes, Ms. Denise Cabbot; very gracious lady. Quite captivating, really."

"You bribed her, didn't you?"

"Well, in a manner of speaking, but I want you to know, she is very good at what she does. When I first approached her, she wouldn't have anything to do with my plan, not until she thoroughly checked my story and verified I was only a slightly sick college buddy with a fondness for playing practical jokes."

"How did you get to her?"

"Well, you know, the MacDougal charm has always been quite an effective negotiating tool."

"When do you pay?"

"Tonight at 8:30. It was a fantastic bit of negotiating. It was a win-win situation. I win by getting in and scaring bejesus hell out of my old buddy, and I win again by having the opportunity to go out with one of God's luscious creatures. Win-win."

"Flip, when will you ever settle down and get serious about your life?"

"Lord willing, never, if getting serious means giving up the pursuit of the fairer sex. It's a MacDougal tradition, one I am only too happy to perpetuate. Besides, my philandering gives you an escape, a release valve. If you didn't have my escapades to tsk-tsk about, you'd have to spend some of your precious research time living your own escapades. So you see, in reality, I'm doing my patriotic duty, keeping you here in this lab coming up with the next...what did you say your project was?"

"Good try, Flip. I didn't, nor will I. How long has it been Flip, two years since the last time you darkened my doorstep?"

'Two years, three months and fourteen days. I counted it up back at the hotel while I was planning this latest mission."

"By the way, where are you staying?"

"At the Triangle Park Radisson in this most sterile of research parks. I must say you have found your element here. I would never have dreamed there could be such a concentration of eggheads in such a folksy state like North Carolina, but The Research Triangle has more eggheads than Perdue has chickens."

"Well, you know you're welcome to stay at my place, although I know you won't."

"That's right. It cramps my style," Flip replied as he pushed off from the counter. "Besides, the Radisson has more than a passable bar and an indoor pool. My suite has its own whirlpool and..." glancing at his watch, "... if I don't get myself on the road, I'll be late for Ms. Cabbot. I know you wouldn't want to be responsible for that."

"You tell Denise she has a lot of explaining to do to one special researcher. It'll be a cold day in hell before I forget the fright you gave me."

"Well, I would imagine despite her taste of the MacDougal charm she might consider making it up to you in some gracious fashion."

"No, no. I know better than that. Once they taste a night of MacDougal, they're never the same, isn't that what you always say."

"Yes, that's true, but I wanted to make you feel better."

Lionel picked up the beaker containing the precious liquid and carefully placed it well out of Flip's reach. "I'll just hang out here in my little dungeon for a few more hours, but will you be around until the weekend?"

"Oh sure, I have a couple of obligations in the evenings but I've reserved the entire day time for my old fraternity buddy. And, by the way, it would appear from your 'dungeon' that my old buddy is doing quite well for himself here at Bio-Tita-Vet."

"Bio-Vita-Tech," Lionel corrected. "And yes, they've been very generous with the grant money. Private industry has certain advantages over the academic scene. Give me a call later. I'd enjoy a weekend of reminiscing. Should I call security to escort you down?"

"No, that won't be necessary. I promise I'll leave straight away." Flip stooped to pick up the briefcase.

"By the way, what's in the briefcase?"

"What's in the beaker?"

"You know I can't tell you that."

"Well then, I'll take the secret of the briefcase to my grave." He grasped the case under his arm securely. "Sure you won't reconsider?"

"I'll pass, thank you. Remember, straight out. If Security catches you sneaking around, they aren't likely to settle for a date with you."

After Flip had left, Lionel returned to his work area. He glanced around the spacious lab at the glistening beakers and the bright lights of the latest, state-of-the-art equipment. Yes, Bio-Vita-Tech had been good to him, and he had returned the favor in kind many times over. He found himself staring at the diplomas over his desk.

Upon each one, in various forms of Old English type was his name, Lionel J. Adams. Fine peasant stock that had made good, he thought, remembering the words his father had used to describe his only son. And now Jacob Adam's son was on the brink of his most brilliant discovery to date.

Lionel lifted the small beaker up to the light and slowly swirled the blue liquid. Perhaps, just perhaps, within the small beaker was the breakthrough Lionel had worked so arduously to produce since his graduation from Duke over seven years ago. Could it be within the molecules of this liquid was the key to unlocking man's true capacity, the ninety to ninety-seven percent of the mind which man had, up to this point in his evolution, been unable to tap? It was too early to be sure, but already there had been some remarkable breakthroughs.

Oh sure, Lionel had had more than his share of setbacks as well. Like the rodents that had been born with enough legs they resembled centipedes, and the guinea pigs that could shatter glass with their shrill whistles. Those had been in the early days, before he had understood the technology of recombinant DNA; not that he completely understood it now, but he was closer.

He now knew for certain that within a special blue-green algae was the raw material of the special template he had been looking for—the template which allowed him to re-structure the DNA molecule, the code of life, to whatever shape and configuration he desired.

Take, for instance, the golden retriever pups he had been working with most recently. Their learning quotient was extraordinary. There was a strong indication they could actually manage rudimentary language differentiation. They were communicating with their trainer. No talking Pluto yet, but not far off.

Lionel placed a stopper firmly into the beaker and walked over to the refrigerator. As he spun the combination on the special lock, he recalled the most recent report that had sent him back to the lab. The retrievers had suddenly developed an aggressive streak that had been unexpected and far from desirable. It appeared, despite their sudden evolutionary leap, there had been an equal reversal to their ancestral tendency to form aggressive packs.

No, the template was not perfected, not quite. He placed the beaker in the special container in the refrigerator and pushed it to the back. Tomorrow he would filter the fluid again to clear it of any possible impurities and run spectrophotometry on it to be sure it had not been contaminated, but for today he was finished. It was getting late, not that Lionel often worried about leaving the lab at any set time. But of late he had started frequenting a small church close to his home, particularly on Wednesday nights during Bible study. If he left now, he'd still have time for a quick dinner before the services began.

Lionel walked to the door. He couldn't explain the reason such a habit had become a part of his life lately, but there was no doubt it was important to him. Few other things could drag him away from his lab at such an early hour. He switched the lights off as he left.

A Message from Orrin Jason Bradford
(a.k.a. W. Bradford Swift)

As an Indie Author I know just how important readers are. Without people who enjoy reading, authors are pretty useless. Oh, I know I enjoy the thrill of writing the *next great American novel,* but that's really not enough. I need readers like you who enjoy reading my stories. So, thank you. I sincerely appreciate your taking the time to read *FreeForm: Resumed.*

Perhaps you would enjoy some of my other books and stories. If you'd like to stay up to date on new book releases, special discounts, and my occasional giveaways, you can also join my **OJB's Amazingly Awesome Readers Group**. Just go to my author's website and blog:

www.wbradfordswift.com

There's one last thing you could do if you would be so kind. Go to your favorite online bookstore and leave an honest review of *FreeForm: Resumed.* Honest reviews are really important to help other readers like you know which books to try next. And thanks for being an amazingly awesome reader.

Orrin Jason Bradford (aka W. Bradford Swift)

Acknowledgments

A very special thank you goes to the 54 Kickstarter Backers that helped fund this book through their kind and generous contributions during my first ever Kickstarter campaign. That in itself probably would never have happened without the prompting of Instafreebie's pilot program, organizer Maura Fertich, facilitator "Obi-wan" Jay Swanson, and the other incredible indie authors of the class. I also appreciate all the assistance from my book cover designer, Victor Habbick and from my editor, Tracy Cartwright. Most of all, I thank my wife, Ann, for always believing in me and bolstering me up with her love and wisdom.

Porpoise Publishing

Flat Rock, NC 28731
www.wbradfordswift.com
Library of Congress Cataloging-in-Publication Data
ISBN: 9781930328846
(paperback)
FreeForm Resumed/ W. Bradford Swift.
1. Science Fiction 2. Speculative Fiction 3. Technology

Cover design by Victor Habbick ~ www.victorhabbickvisions.co.uk/
Typeset in Book Palatino
Printed in USA
First Edition

Also by Orrin Jason Bradford

Fantastic Fables Series
Fantastic Fables of Foster Flat

FreeForm
Crash
FreeForm: Resumed

Saga of the Dandelion Expansion
FreeForm
FreeForm: Resumed

The Cosmic Conspiracy Series
Babble

Standalone
Elliot Savant
Ellenore Finds Her Muse
Stars Beckon Call: A Far Future Dystopian Sci-Fi Thriller

Watch for more at www.wbradfordswift.com.

About the Publisher

Porpoise Publishing is the imprint of indie author W. Bradford Swift who also writes under the pen name of Orrin Jason Bradford. It is best known for publishing visionary fiction--stories that entertain while also inspiring readers to imagine greater possibilities for their lives.

www.ingramcontent.com/pod-product-compliance
Lightning Source LLC
Chambersburg PA
CBHW071344170626
46811CB00003B/975